# Forbidden Brownstones

# Forbidden Brownstones

Clifford Browder

E. L. Marker
Salt Lake City

E. L. Marker, an imprint of WiDō Publishing
Salt Lake City, Utah
widopublishing.com



Cover design by Steven Novak
Book design by Marny K. Parkin

ISBN 978-1-947966-42-0

This book is dedicated to the people of New York.
They are busy, noisy, savvy, creative,
and a bit crazy and wild,
and I love them for all of it.

# 1

IT TAKES AN OBSESSION TO SPICE UP A LIFE, GIVE IT tang and drive. Mine began one day when I was twelve and I was riding with my father in his gig, a light two-wheeled carriage that he delighted to drive about the city in, eyeing the traffic and the crowds. Turning off busy Broadway down a side street, he showed me a long row of houses built smack against one another, all brown, like chocolate cakes squeezed thin.

"See those houses, Junius? Those are brownstones. That's where the gentry live."

I stared in awe. Those were the homes of the white folks who ran the city of New York. From that moment on, those long rows of houses, with stoops rising grandly to majestic portals flanked by tall front windows, struck me as rich, mysterious, and forbidden. I was hooked.

My father was Augustus Caesar Fox, the fanciest barber in the city. He was born a freeman here, since his father, Jeremiah

Fox, a barber in Baltimore, had bought his freedom from his master and moved up here to New York about the turn of the century. My father was also called Dandy Fox because, away from his barbershop, he dressed in the height of fashion and paraded up and down among the fashionables of Broadway, driving a spirited horse hitched to his shiny gig, its top down, and sporting a smart brown frock coat and a well-brushed, tall silk hat. He called this "getting the feel of the town." "There goes Dandy Fox!" the white folks on the sidewalk would exclaim with a smile, thinking he was mocking the uppity fashionables, though I suspect he was up to something else as well: to see if it was safe for him, a black man, to be out and about; my father was no fool.

Poppa's barbershop, on a downtown side street just off Broadway, was fronted by a boldly lettered sign: AUGUSTUS FOX, A KNIGHT OF THE COMB. There, in an immaculate white shirt and black bow tie, he received his customers—merchants, aldermen, bankers, and on occasion the mayor himself—cloaking them in a great white sheet as he trimmed and shaved them in the latest fashion, while offering small talk about anything and everything. So brisk was business, he added two more chairs and hired assistants; his was the premier shop in the city.

When she had errands to do, my mother often left me there. A quiet child, I settled snugly in a corner, content to watch the scene. I remember keenly the *clip clip* of my father's polished silver shears, wielded deftly in an aroma of musk and talcum that blended with the fragrance of fine cigars smoked by patrons awaiting their turn in the chairs. Older, I was allowed to sweep up the shorn locks of the gentry, and when, trimmed and pomaded, they stepped down from the chair, I gave them a quick whisk with a brush, receiving from them a tip of small change with a cheery remark and a smile. When they strode forth from the shop, grasping a cane or a tasseled walking stick and topped by a towering hat, I recognized the strut and scent of power. These were the residents of brownstones, a realization that fueled my obsession even more.

Needless to say, my family didn't live in a brownstone, or in any of the elegant brick row houses that preceded them. They lived in an old frame house on Minetta Lane in Greenwich Village, in the district known as Little Africa. My father and his sisters Bessie and Dilly had grown up there, and there, when he was twenty-six, my father came down bad with a fever, got hallucinations, tossed in bed, and moaned. In the flush of fever he saw a beautiful young black woman standing beside the bed who announced, "I be come to heal you." In his delirium he imagined her hanging bulbs of garlic over his bed, murmuring prayers or incantations, and putting her soft hand on his brow. Finally he drifted off to sleep, and when he woke up, the fever was gone. Standing right there beside him, real as rain, was the loveliest young woman he had ever seen, in a brightly colored patchwork dress, with soft gray eyes that gazed with a soothing warmth.

"You be healed," she said.

Over the bed hung bulbs of garlic.

"You leave them bulbs three days, so as to wind up the work of the healin'. Then you can get up and range about like always."

Before he could speak, she was gone. And he had fallen in love.

Minerva Stokes had never been summoned by the family; she just showed up at the door. She was so soft-spoken and poised that Jeremiah let her in and, at her insistence, left her alone for the healing. It took all of four hours till the fever broke. Jeremiah, retired now and a widower in his sixties, praised the Lord and sent the healer away with a sack of onions, a pink conch shell, and a pair of live trussed geese. "That woman," he told his daughters Bessie and Dilly, "has the Power. She must walk in the light of the Lord."

"But who *is* she?" asked Bessie, a question she'd be asking for years.

Augustus was wondering, too. The moment he got his strength back, he was up and out of there hunting all over Greenwich Village, till he found her living with a bunch of young women in a boardinghouse on MacDougal Street, where he sparked her something fierce till at last she agreed to marry him.

"But mind you, Gus, I've got to be free for the healin'. It's been put on me by the Lord."

They were married in the Greater New Tabernacle Baptist Church, where Bessie and Dilly were members and sang real loud in the choir. Friends of Momma's attended, but no kin. "I comes from far away," she explained; "ain't got no kin in the city." After the ceremony she seemed minded never to set foot in the church again.

"Ain't she a Christian woman?" asked Bessie.

"Seems not," said Dilly.

Himself no churchgoer, my father paid no heed, but it was the beginning of a long to-do.

When they learned that I was on the way, Bessie and Dilly fussed a lot over Momma, asking every five minutes how she felt, if she'd want a midwife to ease the misery, and, when it was time, black pepper tea to bring on the labor.

"Don't need no Bessie or Dilly," Momma told Poppa, "and don't need no midwife neither. Women of my family, we always birth alone." Which was the second and last time she ever mentioned her family.

Years later, Poppa told me how it went. First, Momma had them clear all the "junky stuff" out of the front bedroom—chairs, stools, sharp objects—so as to make for an easy delivery. Then, when her time came, she shooed them all out of the room and walked round and round the bed, holding her belly in both hands. When the pains got fierce, she crept up on the bed, muttered something from Scripture (Poppa heard her through the wall), pushed, and I just popped right out. When they heard my cries, Poppa and his sisters rushed in and oohed and wept for joy, while Momma said over and over, "Sweet Jesus, thanks." And that's how I got born.

Momma named me Junius, which was fine by all. But two years later, when my sister was born—no midwife, just the walk and a push—she named her Angel Blue.

"What kind of a name is that?" said Bessie, out of her hearing.

"Nothin' blue about her," said Dilly. "Like us, she's black as night."

"And to judge by all that screamin'," Bessie added, "she ain't no angel either!"

But Momma had her way. Then, when my sister got out of the toddler stage, Momma started calling her Cecilia, and we all said "Cissy" for short.

After Cissy there were two more births, but the babies died right off. Momma never talked about it; it hurt.

❧

All through the years of our growing, Momma was doing the healing. If any of us got a cut, she used cobwebs to clot the blood; for burns she just laid on her hand, while murmuring some verse from the Bible; and for tummy aches she gave us wild cherry bark tea. All her remedies worked.

Word got round. At any hour of the day or night, black folks would come to see her, and sometimes white folks, too. She saw them in a side room where she had bottles of liquids and powders ranged on a shelf, and sometimes she went down to the cellar, where dried herbs hung from the rafters, and fetched up something that she ground in a mortar and pestle. All through the house there were smells of camphor and ginger and garlic, and other smells I didn't know, some sharp, some soft and soothing. "It stinks in here," said Bessie. "Never mind," said Grandpa Jeremiah. But all too often Momma was called away to see someone sick in bed and might be gone for hours. "She be doin' the healin'," said Poppa, and that was all that mattered. Cissy and I knew that Momma loved us—we could tell it from her warm gray eyes, her soft-touching hands, and the songs she sang us—but she was away a lot and we missed her. Her bright patchwork dresses were known to black folks all over town. "She's a walkin' quilt," said Aunt Bessie, who favored somber dresses all of a hue.

There were seven of us in that house on Minetta Lane, so for a few years we were pretty cramped up. Momma and

Poppa had the front second-floor bedroom, and Aunts Bessie and Dilly shared the other one in back, so Grandpa Jeremiah and Cissy and I had to sleep in the garret. The house had a pitched roof with dormer windows that poked out front and back. Grandpa, a handsome old man of great dignity with tufts of gray-white hair, had a small bedroom facing the yard in back, and snored a lot; Cissy and I each had a small bedroom in front, with a dormer window facing the street. The garret was hot in summer and cold in winter; there were no fireplaces up there, and on frigid mornings the water in the pitchers froze. But we were lucky to have a house of our own. Lots of black people lived thereabouts, to be near their jobs with the white gentry in the fancy houses on Washington Square, but most of them were lodged in seedy boardinghouses that made our house look grand.

After a while both our aunts got married and moved out—Bessie first, then Dilly, since whatever Bessie did, Dilly was sure to follow; I have only a dim memory of the weddings. Grandpa Jeremiah moved down into their bedroom, where his snores still shook the house. He had a way of saying things to me that I only half understood.

"Junius, white folks are strange. It's hard livin' with 'em, but it's even harder livin' without 'em. So, make your peace with that."

"Junius, your momma has the Power. Don't try to understand it; honor it."

"Junius, in this world things ain't what they seem."

"Junius, be strong."

Then he'd stretch out a leg so I could straddle it and play "horsey."

Grandpa Jeremiah walked with a cane but otherwise seemed healthy. So, we were all surprised and shocked when, one warm summer night, he died in his sleep. At the funeral the sisters grieved their hearts out, while Poppa cried softly, holding Momma's hand. For Cissy and me, the only children present, it was awesome. We couldn't get over how Grandpa had always just been there day after day, and now he wasn't, and never would be again. There was a big hole torn in our lives.

❧

At Poppa's insistence I attended the African Free School, where a young black teacher, Mr. Walsh, taught us reading, penmanship, grammar, arithmetic, geography, and a smattering of history. Poppa had had a few years of schooling there; he wanted me to have more. "Education," Mr. Walsh kept telling us, "is the way for our people to raise themselves up out of slavery and its long, dark night of ignorance. You're lucky to be here; think of your brothers in bondage down South. Study hard. Learn!" He kept a hickory switch in the top drawer of his desk, but he didn't need it much; most of us weren't rambunctious. It was there that I first got a taste for reading; books would be important in my life.

Every day Mr. Walsh dinned it into us how we must measure up to the high standard of those who had studied there before us: ministers and educators and successful merchants who made up the city's black elite. This was my first awareness of class within the black community.

"Oh yes," Poppa told me, "there's black gentry—a few—just like the white gentry they imitate. They put on airs and want to lift up all the rest of us and show the white folks what we're worth."

Poppa made it pretty clear that we weren't gentry, and that's the way he wanted it.

Hanging on the schoolroom wall was a big framed print, PARADIGMS OF VICE AND VIRTUE, that Mr. Walsh often referred to with a pointer. In the center foreground was a schoolhouse, and from its door two paths ran out, one to the right and one to the left. The one to the right, "Obedience to Parents and Teachers," led to a steepled church, then past neat little cottages labeled Industry, Faith in Christ, and Humility straight on to the Sweet Waters of Truth and the Mount of Righteousness, where earthbound mortals raised their arms beseechingly toward light shining down from above, where there were soaring angels and the words "Eternal Life."

The path to the left, "Disobedience to Parents and Teachers," meandered past squalid houses labeled Swearing, Lust, Gambling, Intemperance, Fighting, Adultery, and Murder, to a huge, somber building marked State Prison, with a gallows and a dangling corpse beside it. Finally it ended in a blotch of darkness where frock-coated gentlemen and ladies with parasols were hurtled into the bonfire of hell. All in all, I decided that I'd rather take the path to the right.

"Bunkum!" whispered Lester Odysseus Hicks, the boy sitting next to me, who on other occasions whispered "Bosh!" or "Folderol!" or "Piffle!"—all words that fascinated me because I'd never heard them before. A short boy with pointed teeth (rather like a rat's, I thought), Lester interested me, not just by virtue of his impressive full name, or because he was enlarging my vocabulary, but because he kept in his pockets and furtively revealed to me a choice set of marbles, a rabbit's foot, a slingshot, and a rolled-up rubber sheath called the French Secret that he assured me made safely possible the most delectable of pleasures. For Mr. Walsh's Paradigms of Vice and Virtue, he exhibited the utmost contempt.

"All the fun things are on the path to hell. The Eternal Life stuff is a bore!"

Which first planted in my mind, however tentatively, the suspicion that these matters might not be so simple.

On our trips home after school, Lester told me that his father, a coachman, was privy to the secrets of the rich, who did shocking things in private. He often teased me for being such a goody-goody (unlike him, I had never felt Mr. Walsh's switch), then enticed me into games of marbles that, owing to his superior skill, left in his possession the few I had managed to accumulate. For at least one of us, it was a rich and rewarding friendship. A born adventurer, he would be challenging and provoking me for years.

# 2

THE TIMES WERE CHANGING. STARVED OUT OF THEIR island, the Irish were coming over in swarms, pushing black people out of their jobs. The Irish didn't like being called "white niggers"; they thought that if they pushed us down a bit, they'd be climbing up. Poppa had told me more than once, "Wherever you go in this city, look sharp and see if it's safe. If it ain't, get out of there fast!" But you couldn't always sidestep trouble. Going to and from the African Free School, I was called "nigger" or worse. And once, when I was passing a market, an Irish butcher boy sicced his dog on me and laughed as I ran for my life. I didn't much like the Irish.

Then, in the early fifties, Delacorte's Hair Dressing Establishment for Gentlemen opened on Broadway, with chandeliers hanging from a frescoed ceiling, washstands with statuary, giant mirrors, silver toilet services, and a marble floor: luxury that dazzled the city. Within a week or two, all my father's clientele—those elegant residents of brownstones—deserted him for this palatial setting with its team of "coiffeurs," some of whom were actually French. He was stunned.

"Them kwafurs stole my trade!"

Word spread, and soon the more successful black merchants and professionals came flocking to his shop, including Dr. James McCune Smith, the city's first black M.D., who had had to go all the way to Glasgow to get his medical education, and Thomas Downing, whose oyster cellar on Broad Street had been for years a favorite meeting place of the white politicians and money men. So, if Poppa lost the cream of the white clientele, he got the best of the black.

"It's better," he said. "What did I ever get from jawin' with those white muckamucks? I'm with my own folks now, even if some of 'em do put on airs."

With his white patrons gone, I lost my only faint link to brownstones. But I was still thinking about them a lot.

❧

Thanks in part to my schooling, I was going through a phase of asking questions.

"Momma, where are you from?"

"I've told you, child. I be from the mountains."

"But which mountains? Where?"

"Never you mind. I just be from the mountains."

"Why did you leave them, Momma?"

"Because the Lord told me to come here. When the Lord speaks, I don't argue."

About that time Cissy got her courses; I knew because sometimes she'd gasp and wince with pain. Up until then I'd seen her as a runty little thing who teased me; when she did, I called her "Miss Pigtails" and gave them a yank. But now, when Momma told her, "You becomin' a woman," in my eyes she suddenly became a vessel of mystery. For me, women's bodies were a great unknown, a dark tangle of coils and recesses that somehow brought forth life. I was in awe of them.

After that, Momma started whispering to Cissy a lot, and they got to be almighty thick.

"What are you and Cissy always talking about?" I asked Momma once.

"Never you mind. These be women's things. Run along!"

We had a small yard in back with a privy, a well, and a woodshed. Little sun came there, but Momma planted seeds and coaxed up a passel of herbs. Cissy started helping her, and when Momma went on long treks to the north of the city to harvest herbs in the fields, Cissy went along. I was jealous of Cissy already, because she got the other big second-floor bedroom after Grandpa died, while I was still stuck in the garret. Now, being in on things that I was shut out from, she started acting uppity. I complained to Poppa.

"Don't worry about that," he said. "She's young, she'll get over it. This all has to do with the healin'. It's women's work and is passed on from mother to daughter. Cissy's gettin' the fireside learnin' that your momma got from her momma, who got it from her momma, and so on back to Eve."

"Can't I learn some of it, Poppa?"

"Of course not, you're a boy. You're learnin' things at the Free School, and Cissy's learnin' things from her momma. It all evens out."

After that, within one short year both our aunts lost their husbands, Dilly's succumbing to smallpox, and Bessie's to the wide open spaces. "Bessie's man run off," Momma told me, "'cause he couldn't take no more Bessie." So, the two sisters moved in together on Thompson Street, and having no children to keep them busy, came visiting us. Usually they brought a pie or a cake, or preserves that they'd put up, which was fine by me.

"Don't be fooled, Junius," Momma told me after one such visit. "They bring that stuff by way of sayin' to me, 'Woman, why ain't you doin' it, too?' As if I wasn't busy with the healin'!"

If they came when Momma was out, they would talk in front of me as if I wasn't there. Maybe they meant for me to hear, maybe not.

"She always talkin' about bein' from the mountains," Aunt Bessie said once. "Black folks don't live in no mountains. They live down on the flats where the plantations be. Why she talk about mountains?"

"I smell garlic," said Aunt Dilly. "I bet she be hangin' that stuff again in the kitchen. What for? Stink the whole place up!"

"Healin', indeed. There's more than healin' goin' on here. I've heard things."

"What things, Bessie?"

Bessie lowered her voice, but not so much that I couldn't hear. "She lays hants."

Aunt Dilly looked shocked. "How do you know?"

"I got it from Granny Lou, who got it from Eva Ruth, who got it from I won't say who. It's *known*, and Augustus won't do nothin' about it. That man is soft as a cushion. Dilly, we got a conjure woman in the family!"

Aunt Dilly gasped, and Aunt Bessie lowered her voice again to a whisper.

"She be doin' hoodoo next!"

By now, my eyes were big as saucers. But when Momma came back, there was lots of helloing and how-are-you's back and forth, and they were all just smiley smiles.

Later I saw Poppa alone.

"Poppa, what's hoodoo?"

He gave a look. "Who's been talkin' about that?"

"Some boys at school," I lied. "What is it?"

"Just another name for voodoo."

"What's voodoo?"

"A lot of hocus-pocus nonsense way down South. Hexes and spells and suchlike. Nobody up here believes in it."

"Nobody?"

"Nobody in their right mind. See here, Junius, I sent you to the Free School to get some real learnin', so you wouldn't believe in any such nonsense. Forget voodoo and do your sums!"

Easier said than done. When Momma saw a caller in the side room, I started lingering about in the hall outside. There was no door to the side room, just a curtain that Momma pulled shut, so I could hear pretty good. There was lots of talk about aches and miseries, but once an old black woman mentioned a "hant."

"She's a white lady who lived in the house long ago. She keeps comin' back and gives me the creeps. I wants rid of her, Miz Minerva."

"Tell you what," said my mother. "You bring me a chicken or a big china plate, and I'll make you a conjure bag. That'll fix her good."

They went on talking, but Cissy caught me standing there.

"Why are you snooping, Junius?"

"I'm not snooping!"

"You are! I can tell by the look on your face!"

I slunk away. That Cissy knew too much.

All that week I kept an eye out for that old black woman, knowing she'd be sure to come back. When she did, and I knew Cissy was out of the house, I tiptoed up near the doorway and listened.

"What's in it, Miz Minerva?"

"Hog bristles and black cat's hair, a rabbit's foot, and dirt from the graves of three murderers, all tied up in a red flannel rag greased with snake oil, and tied with a dead woman's hair."

"Oh Miz Minerva, that'll do the trick real fine! I give you two china plates for this."

"No, Mattie, I takes only one. But don't open the bag; if you do, the conjure won't work."

Just then I heard the front door open. Cissy was home, so I snuck back to my room in the garret real fast.

Was Momma a conjure woman? Had she really found all those things and put them in that bag? Or was she just hoaxing the old lady a bit, giving her a bunch of nonsense so she'd get over thinking she was plagued by a "hant"? Momma wouldn't flat out cheat anyone, but she might play along with a fancy, aiming to squelch it neat. Which would be a kind of healing. Momma's ways baffled me; I couldn't even begin to find them out.

Just once Lester Hicks said to me, "Junius, your momma's a witch!"

Stung, I lunged at him with such a look of fury that he took to his heels. He never said it again.

# 3

BY NOW THE SLAVERY ISSUE WAS BEING TALKED UP BIG. There were black newspapers that demanded abolition, and when a young black lady schoolteacher tried to ride on a whites-only horsecar and was forcibly thrown off, she sued the horsecar line and won. The judge announced that common carriers had to transport all persons regardless of race. Which meant that when Momma went gathering herbs on the outskirts of the city, she could ride a horsecar or stage much of the way. She couldn't get over it; heady times.

But there were bad things, too. Protected by law, slave-catchers roamed the streets of Northern cities, looking for escaped slaves, and sometimes they grabbed free blacks, too. Black and white abolitionists raised a storm; riots followed.

"Junius," said Poppa, "you're a healthy young black male, just what they want down South. Be careful. You'd fetch a top price in the market."

This stunned me. The thought that I, a free man separated by two generations from bondage, could be snatched off the street and taken down South as a slave, made me for the first time fully grasp the horror of slavery. From then on I carried a knife. Any slavecatcher who messed with me was going to face the fight of his life.

When Poppa was home with us in the evening, sometimes he'd be called away suddenly by a friend, no explanation given. And one Sunday afternoon I saw him and a bunch of his friends marching behind a pine coffin on a wagon, all weeping as they headed uptown. This puzzled me, since up that way there wasn't any black church that I knew of, nor any black cemetery either. But when I asked about it, he put me off.

Years later I learned that Poppa and his friends had been part of the Underground Railroad, putting up fugitives in the basement of the Greater New Tabernacle Baptist Church. This surprised me, because this was Bessie and Dilly's church that he'd mostly kept shy of, except for a wedding or a funeral. "That preacher speaks a hot streak of hell," he'd told me, "and when all them women start hollerin', it kinda wears me down." But it didn't keep him from sneaking slaves in and out of the basement, on their way to freedom far up north in Canada, sometimes in a market wagon with a double bottom, and sometimes in a coffin in a hearse. That's how Poppa was: no agitator, but a quiet doer.

❧

I was out of school now, so it was time I found a job. Poppa had assumed I'd be a barber, too, but when he tried me out, I was clumsy with the shears. "Junius," he concluded, "barberin' ain't for you."

Having other ideas, I'd been intentionally clumsy.

"But what *will* you do?" he asked. "They won't let a black man into most of the trades, and I can't see you as a laborer or janitor or cook. What's left?"

I promised Poppa I'd think about it.

"Well, whatever you decide on, be the best."

That was Poppa's motto: *be the best.*

They still called Poppa "Dandy Fox," and occasionally he still paraded about in his gig to get the feel of the town, though now he wore a smart brown frock coat and a tall silk hat. Gone was the green jacket with shiny brass buttons of his younger days, and I was glad; though I barely remembered it, I suspicioned that it had been just a bit garish. Sometimes I rode with Poppa, all scrubbed up and sideburned, in a tan frock coat and silk hat, with a black satin vest. Easing into early manhood, I wanted to be a dandy, too. Poppa chuckled and approved, and paid for it. And dressing fancy didn't hurt me with the girls; my first adventures date from about this time.

Our promenades were usually up and down Broadway, but on occasion we turned into quieter side streets where the rows of brownstones had started me thinking.

"Poppa, what's a brownstone like inside?"

We were chopping firewood in the yard when I asked; he just kept on chopping.

"How should I know, Junius? I never been inside one."

"Never?"

"Well, almost never. Once, years ago, I was called to one to trim and shave an alderman who was sick in bed."

"What was it like?"

He stopped chopping and thought for a moment. "I can't hardly recollect. Grand, very grand. A marble-tiled floor in the vestibule, and a big canopied four-poster upstairs where his nibs held forth like a king."

"How about the parlor?"

"I just glimpsed it through a doorway comin' and goin'. Chandeliers, as I recall, drapes that made the place gloomy, and a whatchamacallit—pianoforte. But what was really splendiferous was havin' hot and cold runnin' water at a washstand in the bedroom—on the second floor, no less!"

This impressed me, since in our house we pumped water from a well into the kitchen and had to carry it upstairs to the bedrooms. In winter, sometimes that well froze.

"Poppa, do any black folks live in a brownstone?"

"Not that I know of, Junius, not even the ones with money. White folks won't sell to 'em."

"I'd sure like to get inside a brownstone, just to see what it's like."

"Junius, the only way an honest young black man can get inside a brownstone is to become a waiter or a butler."

"What do they do?"

"A waiter waits on the table, just like in a restaurant. And a butler"—Poppa flashed a smile—"well, he buttles. Answers the door, announces visitors, bosses the waiters and maids and cooks. He's the boss man of the servants."

"Then that's what I want to do!"

Poppa didn't look shocked, he just pondered. "Hmm . . . Well, you're well-spoken and educated, and dress well, and it would keep you off the streets. For black people, streets in this city can be dangerous. But you don't just leap smack into it. You'd have to be a waiter first and learn your way around."

"How does one get those jobs?"

"Go to an intelligence office, or answer an ad in the paper. But let me ask my customers. They might put you on to somethin'."

So, Poppa started asking about at the barbershop, where I was still sweeping the floor and whisking off the patrons with a brush.

Meanwhile I was dreaming of brownstone interiors. I'd never seen one, but I'd glimpsed furniture ads in newspapers, fabrics in store windows, and fancy furniture being transported on express trucks in the street. I imagined ceilings as high as a church, chintz and velvet everywhere, fire tongs and mirrors, dainty chairs, whisk brooms with ribbons on them, and hat racks holding clusters of high silk hats. Also, curtsying maids, and a butler in a black frock coat and a white cravat, tiptoeing under chandeliers on rugs so thick you almost lost your shoes in them, as he gave orders to all.

"You understand, Junius," Poppa informed me, "brownstones ain't so different. They're made of bricks, just like lots of other buildings. The brownstone is just for show. It's slapped on the walls facing the street, but underneath there's plain old ordinary brick."

To me it hardly mattered. I knew now that some were called to teach, some to heal, some to snip, some to make money, save souls, or beat the drums for freedom, but I was called to live in a brownstone. Only there would I find out who I was.

Within a week Poppa had a job for me, not in a brownstone but at Downing's oyster cellar on Broad Street.

"You won't be in a brownstone parlor, but you'll see as fancy a place as any in the city. It'll show you how white folks live."

I was thrilled, for this would bring me closer to a brownstone.

Thomas Downing welcomed me, glad to hire the son of his barber. So, for the next two years I was one of three white-smocked young black men knifing open mounds of oysters at a bar near the entrance of Downing's. There, brokers and lawyers and aldermen crowded round at lunchtime, gulping blue points and saddle rocks, while others flocked to the tables, where silverware and crystal sparkled on cloths of spotless white. Gaping at the mirrored arcades, damask curtains, and chandeliers, I revised my vision of a brownstone parlor. Sweeping away whisk brooms and hat racks and other oddments from my father's barbershop, I made it more ornate and grandiose: a cathedral of princely splendor. There, removed from the city's noise and ugliness and danger, even as a servant I could live fancy and walk with dignity and pride.

Circulating among the tables at Downing's was Thomas Downing himself, the richest black man in the city. An elderly man with a close-cropped beard, neatly dressed in a frock coat and a black silk tie, he greeted his white patrons warmly and chatted with them almost as an equal. But remembering my father's barbershop back when his customers were white, I could detect the hint of condescension in the hearty greetings of the patrons, and the barest trace of obsequiousness in Thomas Downing's replies. The game of the two races was played here even more subtly than it had been in my father's shop. Watching, I learned a lot and developed a taste for oysters.

❧

It was Lester Hicks who first gave me a glimpse of the sporting life. He had a job now in a pastry shop on Thompson Street, where he said he was thinking of marrying the owner, a widow. But he also talked about shipping out as a seaman to explore the world's wild and exotic places. With him I visited some dance halls and dives in the Five Points, the city's worst slum, where black men and women rubbed elbows with low-life Irish over penny glasses of rum at the bar. Lester was amused by my astonishment at seeing black and Irish whores hanging out the brothel windows side by side, beckoning to men in the street, and blacks and whites gambling together, and in one dance hall, pipe-smoking colored women and white men dancing a quadrille to screechy music from a banjo, a tambourine, and a drum. Here, among the dregs of society, along streets littered with broken carts, stray bricks, and filth, there was freedom and equality like nowhere else in the city.

Yet these were the blacks that the black gentry shunned most of all: city riffraff who lived low, plus a few newly escaped slaves from the South, raw, loud, ignorant, with the taint of bondage still on them. Free, they were all giving themselves to their pleasures, but at what price? "Things is played out," I heard an old man mutter at a bar, "and I'se about played out, too." These folks weren't going to hell, I concluded; they were there already. I retreated into my brownstone obsession.

One evening when I was at home, Momma suddenly looked Cissy in the eye.

"Gal, you've got yourself into a condition!"

Cissy burst into tears. "Momma, it ain't my fault!"

"No, it never is, now is it? Is he at least the marryin' kind?"

"I ain't never seen him since."

Momma shook her head. "After all I've taught you, you don't know much of nothin'!"

Ever since Cissy had started putting on airs for being in the know with Momma, I'd been calling her Miss Smarty. But now, her sobbing got to my heart.

"This'll be a hard birth," said Momma. "Just wait till Bessie and Dilly get the hearin' of it. Won't there just be a cluckin' of tongues!"

Cissy sobbed harder than ever, but Momma slacked off.

"Never you mind, honey. Your momma'll see you through."

But she was right: Bessie and Dilly, when they heard, clucked their tongues like never before. It was Momma's fault, she'd never had her children baptized, never gave them no raising, was always off "hoodooin' around" when she should have been minding her kin at home. Momma paid no heed, and Poppa didn't either.

When Cissy's time was close, Momma cleared all the clutter out of her bedroom, gave Cissy some raw dogberries to eat, and then some tansy tea to bring on the labor.

"Lord," she said out loud, "give me the mind to know, and the strength to do, so I can birth this baby!"

Then she shooed Poppa and me out of the room and started walking Cissy round and round the bed, just as she'd done when birthing me and Cissy. There was a long wait; Poppa and I paced up and down in the hall. When we heard the baby crying, we both rushed in. There was Cissy, all worn out, with this little black pinch of a baby, all wrinkled and bald, screaming like crazy. "Sweet Jesus, thanks," Momma said over and over.

"Feelin' all right, honey?" Momma asked Cissy later. "No bad headache? No stars thrashin' before your eyes?"

"No, Momma," said Cissy. "I'm fine."

Then Momma motioned me over and gave me a sealed oilskin bag and told me to bury it out back in the yard.

"What is it, Momma?"

"Never you mind. Just sprinkle it with salt, bury it, and bury it deep. Put a big stone on top."

I did it. It was hard work, because the soil was full of rocks.

"That was the afterbirth," Poppa explained. "If anyone or anything messes with it, it might do the mother a hurt."

"Do you really believe that, Poppa?"

"Well, it don't harm none, now do it? She had me do the same thing when you and Cissy were born."

Momma also said to keep the birth fire ashes for a month. Then, three days after the birth, she sprinkled Cissy's clothes with cornmeal bran, and walked her and the baby three times around the yard in back, while singing something I'd never heard before. She called this "takin' the mother up."

Momma was twice glad: first, because the baby was a girl, and second, because it was black like us. Cissy named it Virginia Sweets.

"What kind of a name is that?" Aunt Bessie exclaimed, when she and Dilly came to visit.

"No Christian name at all!" said Dilly.

"No better than Angel Blue," added Bessie, who never forgot a thing.

Cissy wouldn't budge on the name, and Momma backed her up, so Virginia Sweets it was. Like Poppa, both Bessie and Dilly got real fond of the baby and fussed over it no end.

A month after the birth, Momma announced, "The Lord has put on me the burden of catchin' babies. It's an ill convenience, but I don't talk back to the Lord."

So, Momma became a midwife, too. In no time half the black women in the city were coming to her for help. They called her Miz Minerva, then Aunt Minerva, then Granny Minerva.

"They give me all the praises," she said, "'cause I near about know what to do for a lady."

She called it her "Granny work." Her fingers coaxed life; she rarely lost a patient.

# 4

I'VE GOT A WAITER JOB FOR YOU, JUNIUS," POPPA announced one brisk October day after work, "and it's in a brownstone. One of my customers is givin' it up, says you're welcome to it."

My heart leaped. "Where is it, Poppa, and who'll I be working for?"

"A Mrs. Hammond on Seventeenth Street, near the Fifth Avenue. I've got her address. Write her and ask for an appointment. Mention your job at Downing's, and use Mr. Downing as a reference. He won't mind, but ask him first."

I did as Poppa suggested, and within a week I received a scented blue envelope addressed in a slightly wavering hand, with a note inside. At the top of the sheet was a picture of roses and lilies entwined with a ribbon. Under it was the note: "Dear Mr. Fox, please call on me at exactly three o'clock on Thursday next. Sincerely, Amelia Hammond." At the bottom were two pink butterflies.

This was the first letter I had ever received in my life; I was thrilled.

"Wear your best togs," said Momma. "Show the lady you know how to dress."

"But don't climb up the stoop," said Poppa. "Go round to the basement door beneath."

At one minute to three on Thursday, wearing my tan frock coat, silk hat, and black silk tie, I arrived in front of the brownstone on West Seventeenth Street. It was one of a long row of identically fronted residences, differing from the others only in that the tall front windows were shuttered. That array of high stoops looked prodigiously grand. I was far more comfortable going through the area gate around to the basement entrance underneath the stoop, where I knocked. My stomach was aflutter. After years of longing and dreaming, into a brownstone at last!

After a long wait, the door was opened by a young black woman wearing a long white apron over a dark dress, and a white cap with ruffles.

"I have an appointment with Mrs. Hammond."

"Next time use the bellpull." With a slight smirk, she indicated a silver knob dangling from a cord, then waved me in.

I followed her down a corridor and up a flight of stairs. At the top of the stairs a narrow window of multicolored glass filtered light that was blue, red, yellow, and green; it dazzled me. The maid led me to a doorway and announced, "Mr. Fox."

I entered a high-ceilinged room lit by a globed chandelier (gaslight, as I knew from the chandeliers at Downing's), with a marble fireplace whose mantel held a fancy big clock. There were chairs, a table, a desk, sofas, gilt mirrors and pictures on the walls, and a monumental grandfather clock. It was magical, unreal.

Throned in an overstuffed armchair sat a hunched little woman clothed all in black, her gray-silver hair drawn back and massed in a netted bun. She was viewing me through glasses with a long handle that she held before her eyes. As I walked toward her, my shoes sank soundlessly into a thick floral carpet that stretched from wall to wall.

"Stop!" she cried, when I was six feet away. "No closer! Sit in that chair."

Puzzled, I sat on a spindly chair that I feared might collapse beneath me.

"Ordinarily you would not sit in my presence, but an interview is of course an exception. I am Amelia Hammond." She lowered the glasses.

"Good afternoon, ma'am. I am Junius Fox."

"Your note shows excellent penmanship, Mr. Fox. What education have you had?"

Her voice was soft but clear. I noticed a twinkly brooch half lost in the folds of her dress.

"Eight years at the African Free School. I learned penmanship, grammar, spelling—"

"You need not recount all your accomplishments. You are more than qualified for the position of waiter. Your note mentioned a Mr. Downing as a reference. Is that the gentleman of the oyster cellar?"

"Yes ma'am. I've worked there for two years."

"You couldn't have a better reference. My late husband dined there often. Please have Mr. Downing write me."

"I will, ma'am."

"I prefer domestics of your race to these upstarty Irish now flooding the city. I will be in touch with you once I have heard from Mr. Downing. Have you any questions?"

I had lots, but at the moment I couldn't think of one. "No ma'am."

"Very well, then, you may go. Rosalie will show you out. Good afternoon."

With a flick of a black lace fan, she dismissed me. The maid was waiting in the hall, rather close to the doorway, it occurred to me; had she been listening? She led me back to the basement entrance.

"She wouldn't let me get within six feet of her."

"She never will, until she knows you better." We were at the entrance. "Don't get your hopes up, Mr. Fox. She's interviewed five others."

With that, she shut the door.

❧

When I reported the interview to my family, they wanted to know every detail. I described the house, the maid, the parlor, and Mrs. Hammond herself, then concluded, "White folks sure do put on airs!"

"How many in the family?" Poppa asked. "And how many servants in the house?"

I didn't know.

"She a widow lady," said Momma. "Who be lookin' after her affairs?"

"And why wouldn't she let you come close?" asked Cissy. "What's she scared of, anyway?"

They were asking questions I'd barely had time to think about. But having been in a brownstone at last, I was walking on air. Then, doubt seized me: what if I didn't get the job? My stomach clenched. Once I'd asked Mr. Downing to write her, all I could do was wait.

A week later came another scented envelope, this time violet, with a brief note topped by a picture of a little girl sniffing a very red rose, and below, a cluster of blossoms and seashells: "Dear Mr. Fox, please call again at exactly three o'clock on Tuesday next. Sincerely, Amelia Hammond."

"You got the job!" said Poppa. "Why else would she ask you back?"

"I don't know, Poppa. White folks can act pretty strange."

"I'll pray to the Lord," said Momma. "I'll pray you get that job!"

At three o'clock on Tuesday I was at the basement door again. This time I tugged the silver bellpull and heard a faint chime inside. A minute later the maid opened. She had a hint of a mocking smile that told me absolutely nothing. I followed her upstairs to the same room as before and went in. Mrs. Hammond was dressed again in black, sitting regally in the same overstuffed armchair. This time she pointed to a chair about three feet away.

"Good afternoon, Mrs. Hammond," I said as I sat in the chair.

"Good afternoon, Junius."

She looked at me again through the glasses with a long handle that she held before her eyes. On a table beside her, a large album of daguerreotypes lay open.

"Junius, your reference is quite satisfactory. You will be paid six dollars a week, plus room and board. Do you smoke?"

"No ma'am."

"Excellent. No liquor in your room, please, and no visitors. Can you start tomorrow?"

My heart was leaping. "Yes ma'am, as soon as you like."

"Rosalie will show you your room and instruct you in your duties. Somber attire is required; a tan frock coat and plaid vest are much too flash." (I had worn both, hoping to impress her.) "In your room you will find some outfits of Mr. Hawkins, your predecessor. They may fit; if not, they can be altered. Come tomorrow by ten, so you'll be settled in by noon."

Sitting closer this time, I noticed her fine hands with a mesh of tiny wrinkles, and a jeweled ring on one finger. As she talked, under her chin the loose flesh jiggled.

She picked up a silver bell and rang it. The maid appeared: again, a little too soon.

"Please show Mr. Fox his room. Good-bye for now, Junius."

"Good-bye, ma'am. I'm honored to be in your employ."

As I rose to leave, she was turning back to the album. I noticed that most of the daguerreotypes on the open pages had been crossed out with an X in ink.

Humming softly to herself, Rosalie led me up one flight of stairs and gestured toward the bedroom in front. "Mrs. Hammond's room," she explained. Then, up another flight, she indicated two more doors. "This is my room, and that is Mrs. Simmons's, the cook. You'll meet her tomorrow." Finally, up yet another flight: "This is your room here."

"And those rooms?" I asked, having noticed several other doors down the hall.

"Empty."

So, here I was again, alone at the top of the house.

Stepping into the rugless room, I found a bed with straw ticking, a teetery table with chairs, a chipped wardrobe, and a washstand with a basin and pitcher, but no running water.

Brownstone luxury, I realized, stopped on the second floor. Just like in Minetta Lane, I'd be bathing in a tub in the kitchen, probably on a patch of oilcloth spread on the floor. But there was a fireplace with a cast-iron grate heaped high with coal, so when winter came, at least I wouldn't freeze.

Rosalie had entered after me and opened the wardrobe doors. "Here are Mr. Hawkins's things. You'd best try them on for size."

I took off my frock coat and tried on several jackets; to my surprise, they fit. And when I measured some trousers against the ones I was wearing, they seemed to match in length.

"The old gal will be delighted," said Rosalie. "She's pretty tight with her pennies."

"Is she?" I was delighted by this scrap of intelligence.

"She has to be. Her husband was some kind of importer, lost his fortune in that crash in '57. He died soon after, and she's been fighting to make ends meet ever since. Of course all that was before my time."

"How long have you been here, Rosalie?"

She didn't object to my using her first name. "Two years."

"Then how do you know about the crash?"

"Mrs. Simmons. She's been here fifteen years, knows everything."

"Are there any other servants?"

"Just us three. There used to be six or seven, but she had to let most of them go. She kept the coachman until last year, then got rid of him and sold the carriage. For her, that really hurt."

A bell sounded from below.

"She's calling me. We'll have to go."

We retraced our steps to the parlor floor, where Rosalie left me in the hall while she went to attend her mistress. She was soon back and led me down to the entrance.

"Does she spend most of her time in the parlor?" We had reached the door.

"Junius, don't you know anything? That's not the parlor, it's the sitting room. She hasn't used the parlor in years!"

I was on the doorstep. Once again, she shut the door in my face.

*What a saucy little piece!* I thought. *I'll have to take her down a peg, won't I?*

On my way back to Minetta Lane I remembered, in the sitting room, two closed sliding doors with glass windows you couldn't see through, decorated with elaborate designs of leaves. Beyond those doors was the parlor. I longed to see it.

❧

At home the entire family, including Bessie and Dilly, were assembled to hear the news. When I told them I had the job, they all but jumped for joy.

"I knew my boy would get it," said Poppa.

"And look at him," said Bessie. "Ain't he slicked up good!"

They all followed me up to my room and wanted to help me pack, but there was such confusion that I shooed them out, so I could think straight and do it right.

❧

The next morning I moved in. I hired a cart to bring my things, but when Rosalie saw it, she winced.

"Get rid of it as soon as you can! In this neighborhood you don't use carts, you hire an express truck."

Another blunder; I felt small.

Carrying my things up four flights of stairs, and then arranging them in the room, took the better part of the morning. By noon, dressed in a dark jacket and tie, I was down in the basement kitchen, where Rosalie presented me to Mrs. Simmons, a stout black woman of fifty who gave me a quick friendly nod, then turned back to her stove. It was my first sight of a cookstove, a huge contraption fitted into a gaping fireplace, with a box for coal beside it; at home, my mother cooked in an open hearth. I was beginning to realize how backward our arrangements were, how mean, how crude.

"Miz Hammond dines promptly at one," Mrs. Simmons announced. "You will serve her."

The dining room, I gathered, was the back room on the parlor floor, just overhead.

"So, I'll tote the trays upstairs?"

Mrs. Simmons smiled, Rosalie laughed.

"Oh Junius," said Rosalie, "you've got so much to learn! There's a dumbwaiter!"

She opened a panel in the wall, revealing a platform with a rope pulley. Tugging on the rope, she caused the platform to soundlessly rise.

"Mrs. Simmons puts the trays here, and they're lifted up to the butler's pantry, where you'll receive them. Come, I'll show you."

She led me up to the parlor floor and showed me the butler's pantry, a small room behind the stairs, next to the hall door leading to the dining room. Besides the dumbwaiter opening, there was a counter holding—she pointed them out in turn—cruets of oil and vinegar, a mustard pot, salt and pepper shakers, a breadboard and knife, bottles of sauces and spices, and a stack of trays.

"The main thing is to keep the food hot. Now come in here and I'll show you how to set the table."

We entered the dining room, another high-ceilinged space with a gas-lit chandelier, a shiny white marble fireplace, a sideboard with sparkling crystal and stacks of fine china, a long table and chairs, and dark green velvet wallpaper that I couldn't help but caress: it was sensually smooth and soft.

"Junius!" cried Rosalie. "Pay attention!"

She was taking a napkin and silverware from the sideboard and arranging them at the head of the table. Only one chair, high-backed and thronelike, was drawn up.

"There!" said Rosalie. "That's how it's done!"

I tried to focus on the setting, but already my eye was straying to a large bay window, bathed in sunlight, that looked out on a garden in back. Compared to this room, the sitting room was dim and shabby. And I had yet to see the parlor!

At one o'clock Mrs. Hammond entered the dining room, walking slowly with a tasseled cane. Instructed by Rosalie, I was there to seat her at the head of the table; she nodded and sat. With Rosalie whispering to me in the pantry, I served each course as it arrived in the dumbwaiter: a brown soup that Mrs. Hammond sipped with a glass of sherry; a slice of roast with mushrooms and asparagus; a green salad and a dish of blue cheese; and finally, a sliver of cake and tea. Throughout, I stood silently a few steps behind Mrs. Hammond, out of her sight but within easy call, removing each course's dishes before serving the next. Of course I made mistakes: I served the salad on the left, not the right; fetched a spice bottle when she asked for vinegar; and almost spilled the tea. Through it all she remained unruffled, correcting me firmly but courteously, with never a trace of temper. The sight of her at the head of a long, empty table, dining fastidiously in silence, impressed me; she had dignity.

Later, after she retired to the sitting room, and the dirty dishes had been lowered to the kitchen, Rosalie and I joined Mrs. Simmons in the kitchen for lunch. Minus the sherry, we had the same food as our mistress, less fancily served; I'd never dined so well. Being new, I kept mum and listened as Mrs. Simmons wondered about who was moving in next door, and Rosalie prattled about the latest murder reported in the papers.

"Get your apron, Junius," said Rosalie as we got up from the table. "We're going to do some dirty work now."

In all my fantasies of brownstones, I had given little thought to the kitchen, and none at all to the furnace room. Now, fetching from my bedroom a long black apron with thin white stripes that I had inherited from Hawkins, I went with Rosalie into this unknown realm. Next to the kitchen, I learned, was a laundry room, and down another flight of stairs was a cavernous cellar, cool and dark, where Rosalie lit a lamp that cast a feeble light.

"Those bins over there," she explained, "are for storing vegetables and fruit. That closet is for meat and poultry. And this thing over here"—she indicated a bulky iron structure encased in a thick brick vault—"is a hot-air furnace."

The massive shape radiated heat; a coal bin sat beside it. She opened a small door in the furnace; inside, ruddy coals glowed a heat that singed my face. She shut the door.

"See those tin pipes? They carry the hot air up to the parlor floor, where it goes out through vents in the walls."

"Then what are those fancy fireplaces for upstairs?"

"Those marble things?" She laughed. "They're just for show."

I recalled Grandpa Jeremiah's words: "Things ain't what they seem."

All through the winters of my childhood, I had clung to blazing wood-fire hearths, then trudged upstairs to a frigid bedroom. Now, that was over. Even if the hot air from the furnace didn't reach to my bedroom here, the coal grate would give out a good, steady heat. And on the lower floors where I would be working, cold was banished from all but the remotest crannies and nooks. Despite all the upstairs splendors, maybe the greatest wonder of a brownstone was this dirty coal-eating monster hidden away in the bowels of the cellar, generating the miracle of warmth.

Rosalie showed me how to stoke the furnace with coal, and promised future lessons in how to bank the cinders at night, and how, in the morning, to rake out and dispose of the ashes. All these tasks were mine, plus carrying coal upstairs to the kitchen and bedrooms in a scuttle.

"And the sooner you learn, the better," said Rosalie. "I hate coming down here. Look at us, we're smirched!"

It was true: just from stoking the furnace, our hands and aprons were smudged black. This at least we could agree on. But from then on it was war.

# 5

UNDER ROSALIE'S GUIDANCE, OVER THE NEXT FEW days I learned to rake out the furnace and stoke it with coal in the morning; to take ashes out to the curb for collection; to bring slop jars down three and four flights from the bedrooms, and tote up water and coal; to clean chimneys of kerosene lamps and trim their wicks (no gaslight above the second floor); to set the table for Mrs. Hammond's breakfast, lunch, tea, and supper, serve her, and stand by while she dined; to polish brass andirons in those shining fireplaces devoid of heat; to rub tables with oil. My day began an hour before Mrs. Hammond rose at eight and ended an hour after she retired, which put me in bed toward eleven. Whatever gritty labor was to be done, I did it, traipsing up and down stairs all day. Meanwhile Mrs. Simmons cooked and washed dishes in the kitchen, and Rosalie saw Mrs. Hammond up in the morning, helped her downstairs, polished plate and silver, lightly dusted surfaces with a feather duster, and lorded it over me:

"Junius, you forgot to take the coal to the bedrooms!"

"Junius, there's trash to be taken out to the curb!"

"Junius, this lamp isn't clean! I've told you how to do it twice!"

Yes, war. A war fought with kerosene lamps and slop jars and cruets, with coal scuttles and trash. But the more she scolded me, the more I was determined to persist. She wasn't born in a brownstone either. I'd show this little smarty I could learn just as much as she had, and more. As for taking her down a peg, that would have to wait.

Within the first month I had mastered a whole new vocabulary: whatnot, antimacassar, cruet, lorgnette, reticule, commode, and rosette; words that I whispered in a litany of love. I knew that the parlor-floor woodwork was black walnut, the shutters mahogany, and Mrs. Hammond's desk in the sitting room rosewood, and reveled in their woody presence. I had had the exquisite pleasure of stroking brocade and velvet, yearned to touch damask and tulle. I knew that Mrs. Hammond wore sometimes a necklace of pearls, sometimes a beryl brooch, and I longed to experience the glinty magic of topaz, amethyst, and jet. No matter how Rosalie bossed me, no matter what work they put upon me, and no matter how plain my room, each day of my life I was immersed in luxury and taste. The smells of the house were perfumes. At every opportunity I caressed each fabric, each surface, as if it were a woman's warm flesh.

❧

Thursday was my day off; leaving after breakfast, I saw my family at home and regaled them with tales of the brownstone. Poppa marveled at the hot-air furnace; Momma and

Cissy loved to hear about Mrs. Hammond's fancy dining and jewels; and Bessie and Dilly thought a flush commode (to which only Mrs. Hammond had access) a miracle worthy of the Lord.

"That is some livin'!" said Bessie.

But when I ate with them, I was embarrassed. They used a knife, not a fork, to eat vegetables; didn't break bread, just bit into it; slurped soup with their nose in the bowl; and blew on their coffee to cool it. I said nothing, but having watched Mrs. Hammond dine, I could never eat like my family again. As for our furnishings—some bought, some scavenged, all basic, nothing stylish—they now looked like a hodgepodge of junk.

Thursday afternoons I did errands, visited an African book-lending society to replenish my reading, and got the feel of the town. If I met some chum from school or Downing's, we'd go for a mug of beer or ale, but most of the places catering to blacks were dingy bars in the Five Points that struck me as crude and depressing. If I was seeing a girl, I might take her down to the Battery for a fine view of the harbor, its waters plied by vessels with puffed white sails, smoke-belching steamboats, and small craft, or to the pastry shop on Thompson Street where Lester Hicks used to work, until he got bored and left.

I'd been out of touch with Lester for a year, when I bumped into him on Broadway. He was wearing a high beaver hat and suspenders like workmen wear on the docks. Eyes glowing, he had tales to tell.

"I did it, Junius! I shipped out to the Caribbean on a schooner that brought back hogsheads of molasses, and these huge, almost man-sized turtles that make the best soup you ever tasted. Junius, it's a dream come true to walk naked in the fine white sand of those beaches, looking for Spanish doubloons, and then to swim in the warm, blue sea. Down in those islands you'll find the gentlest breezes and the most voluptuously willing women who know ways of love you never imagined. But you've got to be careful: sharks cruise in the surf, tarantulas crawl out of bunches of bananas, and if you walk under the palm trees, you might get konked by a coconut."

His stories were stupendously vivid and grand, but I had my brownstone, and no, I wouldn't lend him five dollars.

Mrs. Simmons had Sunday off, so she could go to church; she prepared breakfast before departing, left food in the kitchen that Rosalie could heat up and serve. Rosalie's day was Saturday, and I welcomed it as giving me relief from my mentor tormentor. One Saturday morning I saw her in the hall as she was leaving. Gone were the house cap and apron. Instead, she was wearing a beribboned bonnet with a dotted veil, a lavender dress with a white ruffed collar and cuffs, and a black belt with a gold buckle, and held a parasol tightly furled. No young woman in the city could have looked more elegant. Up until then I had considered her a pert little number, nothing more. Now, I couldn't help wondering to what other life she was going.

Since it was my job to clean out and replenish the coal grates, I had access to the help's rooms during the day. Mrs. Simmons's was predictably bare, with a lone geranium on the windowsill, a black-bound Bible on a table, white wool stockings draped over the back of a chair, and smells of soap and camphor. In Rosalie's room I had noticed little more: a rag doll on the bed, a green hassock, a cluttered dresser top, a wardrobe emitting a scent of lavender. Now I was suddenly curious.

That afternoon, on the pretext of cleaning the grate, I quietly entered her room. Opening the wardrobe doors, I found another bonnet and a small hat hanging on pegs, garments folded flat on shelves, and ranged on the bottom, several pairs of high-topped patent-leather shoes much too fancy for a maid.

Next, the dresser top drew me: a comb and brush, a small mirror that tilted in its frame, a red pincushion with every kind of ornamental pin, and a cut-glass bottle with a stopper giving out an intoxicating fragrance. By now, I was seduced. Amid this charming clutter stood the full-length photograph of a young black man in a dark top hat, white stand-up collar, dark jacket with a white carnation in the lapel, and leggings tucked in high black boots: the uniform, as I knew from forays with my father in his gig, of a coachman or groom of the wealthy. At the sight of this liveried flunkey, I felt a flash of jealousy.

Silently, I opened the dresser's top drawer, reveled in its contents: a rainbow of ribbons, a wooden dish with buttons of every size and hue, loose buckles, silver shears like those my father used in his shop, hairpins, measuring tape, thimbles and spools of thread, scraps of velvet, tucks and tufts of lace. There were gloves whose scent enthralled me, and in a little painted box, a brooch; I fingered its hard glitter. The whole array was subtly, exquisitely sensual.

Though tempted to explore the other drawers, I didn't. She was presumably gone for the day, but could, after all, return at any moment. Already I had amassed more than enough fuel for my fantasies. Checking to make sure that I had left everything exactly as I found it, I withdrew, and for days afterward dreamed of her decked out with ribbons and lace, her gloved hands scented, her whole getup emitting the smooth, hard glitter of her brooch. At the very thought of her, my doodle stood to attention.

❧

Though her mocking smile persisted, Rosalie's scoldings gradually diminished. She had to admit that I now knew a cruet from a salver, could trim lamp wicks efficiently, and coax the most reluctant coals to life. To further improve my image, when I set out for my Thursday off, I made sure she saw me in a well-brushed topper, a black silk cravat, an imitation diamond tiepin, check trousers, and pearl-gray gloves. Tit for tat: let her wonder what *I* was up to.

If she did, she gave no sign. At our communal meals in the kitchen, she talked only of trivia: fires, pickpockets, murders; where the best oyster stands were located; the chic of dotted veils. This bored me. Mrs. Simmons, on the other hand, could be a fund of information.

"Miz Hammond has had trouble a-plenty. Lost her husband, her son, and all kinds of other kin as well."

"Is that why she puts X's on all those pictures?" I asked.

"That's her way of grievin', though I don't see that it do her much good."

"Isn't there a married daughter up in Boston?" asked Rosalie.

"Yes, and with three young chillen, but Miss Clara hardly never visits down here, treats her momma so miserable mean. Some old quarrel between them, I guess. Miz Hammond just sits in that sittin' room with her albums and letters and such right into the pink of the evenin', rememberin' all the years behind her. She's just lonesome to death. Poor lady—all alone."

Which were exactly my momma's words, when I told her of Mrs. Hammond's dining at the head of an empty table: "Poor lady—all alone."

Twice a week Mrs. Simmons, having consulted Mrs. Hammond after breakfast, sent me out to do the marketing. Mrs. Hammond's list was very precise, with the address of the butcher or grocer, and a price for each item indicated.

"Don't you never pay more," Mrs. Simmons told me, giving me just enough cash. "Miz Hammond is a sparin' woman."

Being the son of another "sparin' woman" who had taught me to haggle at the market, I soon found that, by going down to the Jefferson Market at Sixth Avenue and Greenwich, I could beat the prices of the local shops. I might easily have pocketed the difference; instead, I returned the savings to Mrs. Simmons, who scrutinized the meats and produce, approved of them, and marveled.

After several weeks these savings of a few pennies here and there began to add up. One afternoon Mrs. Hammond summoned me to the sitting room, where she was seated at her rosewood desk, bent over a ledger.

"Junius, your shopping has been most economical, and your performance in general quite satisfactory. I hope that you will continue in my employ for a long time to come."

I was elated. "Thank you, ma'am. I hope so, too."

I enjoyed those forays to the market, a wicker basket on my arm. Coming back, I was enveloped by silence. Thick walls and the shuttered front windows kept out all the ruckus of the city. On the parlor floor our steps were muffled by thick carpets, and even on the uncarpeted stairs and in the hallways, everyone seemed to tread lightly. Voices were never raised, loud anger was unheard of. We moved in the softest gaslight; only the dining room, with its bay window facing south, received the glare of the midday sun, against which drapes were drawn. By day as by night, we lived in the muted gloom of a white folks' church, so different from the constant commotion I had grown up in on Minetta Lane. Silence and elegance had become my need, my home. Thanks to them I felt removed not only from my family, but from the low-life blacks I saw on the streets: the sawyers and chimney sweeps and peddlers, the drunks and whores of the Five Points, the tubmen carting away the waste of the white folks' privies at night. Shunning them, I felt more genteel, quieter, cleaner, and just a tiny bit elite.

One morning Mrs. Hammond came downstairs in a very full lavender dress trimmed with black braid and white lace; it was striking.

"Mrs. Hammond," I said, "please don't think me forward, but that dress is most becoming."

Her eyes flashed, her soft voice stabbed. "Junius, it is not for you to pay me compliments!"

I was crushed. "Excuse me, ma'am. I forgot myself."

Not another word was spoken. To end the awkward silence, I left, then brooded all day, obsessed by my transgression. I still had so much to learn!

That evening she summoned me to the sitting room. "Junius, I spoke harshly this morning. I apologize."

"That's quite all right, ma'am. I was out of line."

"No, you were not. I am an old woman, dried up at heart and bitter. I have forgotten how to receive a compliment. Forgive me."

"Mrs. Hammond, that's quite all right."

Neither of us ever mentioned the incident after that, but never again did I venture to pay her a compliment.

# 6

Mrs. Hammond had worn the lavender dress that day, I suspected, because her lawyer was going to call. She received just three visitors: her lawyer, her physician, and her minister, all garbed in black, though the lawyer often sported a crimson tie.

"If the old gal's seeing her lawyer," Rosalie informed me, "that means there's money problems again. She'll be selling something more from the house."

The following morning Mrs. Hammond called me to her rosewood desk in the sitting room, handed me a card:

**NOAH P. WHIPPLE**
*Broadway & Houston*
*Expert Carting*
*No job too big or too small*
*Special springs for delicate operations*

"Junius, please inform Mr. Whipple that I will require his services on Friday at eight a.m. He will know what arrangements to make."

I did as instructed. When I told Rosalie, she smiled.

"She always has him come early, so as to get the stuff away before the neighbors are up and about."

At eight on Friday Mr. Whipple, gray-smocked, lean, and wiry, and wearing a stovepipe hat, had his cart at the curb outside, with a young Irishman to assist him. Helped by me, they gently tipped the grandfather clock in the sitting room and carried it gingerly out the front door and down the stoop to the cart, and secured it there with ropes. Having always been fascinated by the clock, with its black hands pointing to gold numbers on a silver face, and its pendulum and wheels visible through a glass-plated front, I gave a last touch to its rich woody surface just before the cart drove off. Mrs. Hammond never mentioned the clock again, but a large empty space in the sitting room bespoke our loss.

❧

When her doctor visited, they were closeted together in the sitting room for about a half hour; after he left, she was always out of humor.

"Junius, beware of physicians. They take your money and give you nothing. Humbugs!" With surprising force, she slammed her fist on the desk.

"You're not feeling well, Mrs. Hammond?"

"Of course I'm not feeling well! At my age, what can you expect? I have a cough that persists, and every muscle in my body aches."

"My mother could help." The words were out of my mouth before I knew it.

"What did you say?"

"My mother's a healer. She could help."

"A healer? I've never heard of such a thing."

"It's an old tradition among our people, passed down from mother to daughter. Momma uses sassafras tea for coughs, and rhododendron oil for aches."

"And it works?"

"Usually; not always."

"Hmm . . ." She pursed her lips, thought. "It's quite out of the question. Dr. Bowers would never approve."

"Momma has helped a lot of folks who can't afford a doctor."

"Quackery!" she exclaimed, which ended the discussion.

When I left her, she was coughing, and rubbing an achy arm.

For Christmas Mrs. Hammond put up no decorations, but gave us each an envelope containing five dollars—for her, a sacrifice—and let us have the day off. Mrs. Simmons stayed with her, having nowhere else to go, and I went to my family. Rosalie seemed to have no family, but she left in the height of fashion, probably to celebrate with her liveried flunkey.

"What did Mrs. Hammond do on Christmas Day?" I asked over breakfast the following morning.

"What she always does," said Mrs. Simmons. "Stayed in bed all day."

"The whole day?"

"The whole day. Had a little toast and tea for supper; I took it up. But now that it's over and done with, she'll be up and about like always."

"I hope so," said Rosalie. "But who knows? When I put her to bed at night, she never lies down, always sleeps propped up with pillows."

"Why?" I asked.

"Scared."

"Of what?"

"Of death," said Mrs. Simmons, who promptly changed the subject.

I thought about it afterward, remembering Mrs. Hammond's fear of strangers, the house's dim lighting and silence, the shut-off parlor, the crossed-out photographs. Also, by now I'd noticed that some of the drapes were faded, much of the upholstery worn. And in the little hallway windows that charmed me with their play of multicolored light, some of the tiny panes were missing, replaced by ordinary glass. Decay was all around. Was my brownstone a mansion of death?

❧

Mrs. Hammond was indeed up and about the next morning; for her, Christmas was a one-day ill.

In January she invited her minister to tea, a ritual that she observed punctually every three months. The Reverend Timothy Blythe, D.D., as he announced himself with a card, was the rector of the Church of Christ and All Angels on the Fifth Avenue, which Mrs. Hammond used to attend, when she still had her carriage. Now she couldn't go to him, but he still came to her, a tall, brisk man, richly sideburned with brilliantined hair, a gold ring on one finger, and stylishly dressed. She received him in her armchair in the sitting room, before a low table where I placed a polished silver tray with a silver tea set and a dish of crumpets and scones.

"My dear, my very dear Mrs. Hammond!" he exclaimed by way of greeting, bowing to kiss the jeweled finger of her extended hand. "How are you on this fine January day?"

"Awful. Please sit and have some tea."

"Gladly. Your tea is always delectable, and your scones superb. Shall we pray a bit?" He winked.

"Certainly not; the tea will get cold. So, what have you to tell me?"

"Tidbits galore: a vestryman's indiscretions, my brilliant snagging of a wealthy new parishioner from Trinity, a soprano's disgrace."

"Excellent! Start with the most scandalous."

Just as the conversation was getting interesting, Mrs. Hammond waved me away.

Rosalie was waiting in the hallway with her usual hint of a smirk. "They'll be at it for an hour," she whispered. "Come."

Putting her finger to her lip, she beckoned me to the stairs and started up, always motioning me to follow. This surprised me, since lately she had been unusually distant and elusive. Upstairs, she stopped in front of Mrs. Hammond's door, put her finger again to her lips, waved me in. Since the room was heated with hot air from the furnace, there was no coal grate to clean; I'd been in it only once, taking a tray to Mrs. Hammond on a Saturday, when Rosalie was off, and chiefly remembered how shrunken Mrs. Hammond looked, alone in the huge four-poster bed. Of course I longed to visit that room again. Had I asked Rosalie to let me see it, she would have refused with a smirk. Since I hadn't asked, she ushered me in. I felt a tingle of excitement.

The bed was indeed huge, under a fringed canopy; I caressed the thick quilt, felt the laced pillowcases. Rosalie beckoned me to the dressing table, with its stoppered bottles and little boxes emitting hints of perfume and talcum and soap, backed by a spotless mirror.

"Rice powder," she whispered, pointing. "Cucumber cream . . . rose water . . . chalk . . . But you should see her without her teeth!"

I reveled in all these secrets of our mistress's toilette. Then she opened a sandalwood box containing a cluster of fans and flicked each one open in turn:

"Carved ivory . . . tortoiseshell . . . lace . . . mother-of-pearl . . ."

This last one fascinated me with its ivory-white iridescence tinged with a hint of blue. But when I started to stroke it, she flicked it shut.

Next, she tiptoed to a dresser, pointed to a large gilt box whose glass-covered lid pictured a lady of another age in a towering wig with plumes, primping before a mirror in her boudoir, flanked by naked cupids. Raising the lid, she revealed several rows of rings and jeweled pins, all of different colors and glinting, secured in little slots on a background of black velvet. She whispered their names like magic:

"Sapphire . . . diamond . . . amethyst . . . topaz . . . coral . . . jet . . ."

The incantation enthralled me. But then she touched several empty slots in turn:

"Pawned! The old gal's stretched to the limit."

I reached to touch the gems, but she shut the lid, almost catching my fingers, and waved me toward the door. I took a last look at the forbidden chamber, and then we tiptoed out.

Downstairs, peals of laughter came from the sitting room. It was the first time I had heard Mrs. Hammond's laugh; it sounded musical and young. When the reverend left her, their eyes were bright with mirth. A mansion of death indeed!

❧

Going up to my room that night, I happened to meet Rosalie coming from Mrs. Hammond's room, where she had seen the old lady into bed. We climbed another flight together, paused outside Rosalie's door. Remembering the reverend's gallant gesture in greeting Mrs. Hammond, I took Rosalie's hand and raised it to my lips. She snatched it away.

"No foolishness!"

I smiled. "Why not?"

"Mrs. Simmons is right there through that door," she whispered.

"So what? She can't see us."

"That's what *you* think! Why did you get your job? Because Luke Hawkins had liquor in his room. How did Mrs. Hammond find out?" Wordlessly, she gestured emphatically toward Mrs. Simmons's door. "She's the old gal's eyes and ears. She knows *everything!*"

With that, she darted into her room and shut the door.

In my own room one flight up, I coaxed flames from the coal grate, pondered. Rosalie—delicious, mocking Rosalie—was afraid of Mrs. Simmons! This changed everything. I recalled a conversation with my father just after I got the job.

"Junius, look close and see who has the power. In every home, like in every shop or business, someone has the power. Here, it's your momma, and I don't mind, 'cause it's a healin' power. In that brownstone someone has the power; find out who it is."

"Mrs. Hammond has the power, Poppa. She's the boss lady, after all."

"Maybe, maybe not. Often there's power just lyin' about unused, waitin' to be grabbed. The bosses don't always notice, sometimes don't even care. But someone will grab that power. Make sure that it's you."

When I began my job with Mrs. Hammond, I assumed that Rosalie had the power, since she ordered me around. Since then, as I learned the ropes, her power had diminished. Now I began to take a fresh look at Mrs. Simmons, this dowdy old woman, barely literate, who mostly kept to her kitchen, scraping carrots, stirring soups, then in off moments quietly read her Bible (she had one in her room, another in the kitchen), but at our communal meals suddenly gushed information that she'd then cut off like a tap. Up until now I'd dismissed her as just another old darky woman one step removed from the plantation. But now I'd have to take her seriously: she had the power.

# 7

IT WASN'T ALWAYS LIKE THIS. TIME WAS, SHE AND Mr. Hammond were real sociable, had friends just any-wheres about. On New Year's Day, when Mr. Hammond went out callin' and she stayed home to receive, all the gentry wore a slick path to her door—bankers and judges and all kinds of muckamucks. That parlor was fixed up fancy with ferns and vines in the windows, whatnots with brickybrac, and a mantel clock that struck the hour and out come these little figures just as cute as you please. Oh, it was a sight to see!"

When Mrs. Simmons reminisced in the kitchen, I knew by now to just let her talk. If questioned, she might clam up.

"But those days are a nigh-gone thing. That crash came, and whoosh went their money, and soon afterward Mr. Hammond got down sick and died. Oh, she loved him a heap. She just grieved and grieved, shut up that parlor, and it ain't been opened since."

Hearing Mrs. Simmons talk, I conceived a burning need to see the parlor, the only room I hadn't as yet explored. The parlor was where brownstone residents put themselves most splendiferously on display. It was reserved for formal visits and special occasions like weddings and funerals. Through those shut sliding doors with frosted glass windows that I saw every day in the sitting room lay the house's holy of holies, a forbidden and coveted realm. Only when I penetrated there would I truly know this brownstone, probe its mysteries, pierce its sensual depth.

"Have you ever been in the parlor?" I asked Rosalie in the hallway.

"Just once, when the old gal had me fetch her out a hassock."

"What's it like?"

"All shrouded and dim. Everything under dustcovers. Nothing much to see."

"Well, I want to see it."

"You go in there, it could cost you your job."

"Maybe someday when she stays in bed feeling poorly."

"Mrs. Simmons would know."

"On a Sunday when she's off."

"What would you do in there?"

"Look at it. Feel it. Possess it."

"You're crazy."

"Wouldn't you like to see it with the shutters open and light pouring in? It would be a feast, a fulfillment."

"You're crazy."

"If Mrs. Hammond decides to stay in bed all day on a Sunday, promise you'll let me know right off."

"I don't want to lose my job."

"You won't. Be a sport. Promise."

"Oh, all right. But I'm not going in there with you."

"Of course not." I smiled.

It was a long wait. Whenever Mrs. Hammond felt under the weather and clung to her bed, it was never a Sunday; my patience began to wear thin. Then one day it occurred to me that, on my own floor, I had never explored one of the unoccupied bedrooms in back. That evening, kerosene lamp in hand, I pushed the door quietly open and went in.

What I found were toys, neatly arranged on the bed, the dresser, and the floor. Wooden soldiers with tall black hats; a big horse on wheels that a child could lead about or ride; a drum; a zebra and a giraffe; a steamboat that you could wind up and make run on the floor. Toys like I had never had. Her dead son's toys, dusty, untouched for years. I blew dust from the soldiers, admired their uniforms; pushed the wheeled horse; wound the steamboat up and sent it creeping across the floor. Why were they still here? After all this time, couldn't she let go? Strange. I tiptoed out.

Finally, one Sunday in March, Rosalie whispered to me in the hallway, where I was toting out ashes from the grates. "She's ached up, says she won't be down all day."

A thrill ran through me: at last! "After lunch, when the light in there will be best."

"I'm not going in."

"Of course not."

After lunch we entered the sitting room. Trembling slightly, I eased the sliding doors open and, lamp in hand, looked in. Rosalie was right behind me. Shapes loomed on all sides, shrouded in dustcovers. Quietly I advanced, my steps muffled by thick carpeting, then opened the heavy drapes of the two front windows as gently as I could, so as not to raise clouds of dust. Unlatching the mahogany shutters, I pushed them open. Light flooded the room, revealing a chandelier with crystal pendants suspended from a sculpted rosette in the ceiling, and ornate molding along the tops of the walls. There was a pure white marble fireplace topped by a mantel with a large bronze clock flanked by candelabras, and backed by the largest mirror I had ever seen. Rosalie and I both stared.

On the wall opposite the fireplace hung two full-length oil portraits in thick gilt frames. Looming out of a black background in one was a mature woman in a blue ball gown with white ruffles and white lace sleeves, her arms and shoulders bare, a pink rose in her bosom; in her hand was a black lace fan I recognized. In the other frame stood a tall, straight-spined older man, clean-shaven and sideburned in the style of the fifties. He was wearing a dark frock coat over a patterned waistcoat and a ruffled shirt with a black cravat. Both portraits breathed dignity and wealth.

"Weren't they something!" whispered Rosalie.

"Magnificent! Worthy of their brownstone."

Folding the dustcovers gently back, I peeked at damasked chairs with delicate curved legs, an ottoman with needlepoint cushions, a bust on a pedestal, a labeled marble sculpture: Mounted Amazon Attacked by a Tiger. Unveiling a pianoforte, that hallmark of white gentility, I touched a key, produced a resonant note.

"Hush!" whispered Rosalie.

On a separate stand lay a thick-bound, gilt-edged Bible, open to a page topped by an engraving of a half-draped urn labeled DEATHS, with a downcast angel beside it, and flanked by weeping willows. My eye went at once to the last entry at the bottom of the page: "Paul Gardner Hammond, son of Wilbur F. and Mary G. Hammond, February 2, 1858, heart trouble, 62 years, 4 months, 5 days." Though it was firmer then, I recognized her hand.

Scanning the other entries—parents, sisters, cousins of the husband, numerous infant mortalities—my eyes fixed on an item near the top, in a faded script that was new to me: "James Frederick Hammond, son of Paul G. and Amelia J. Hammond, June 12, 1836, pneumonia, 10 years, 3 months, 2 days." This was Mrs. Hammond's son, the Master Jim that Mrs. Simmons had spoken of. A wave of pity swept over me, a feeling of futility and loss.

"Let's get out of here," whispered Rosalie. "It's beginning to give me the creeps."

We pulled the dustcovers gently back down, shut and latched the shutters, closed the drapes. Just then the clock on the mantel struck two. As I held up the lamp, moving out from either side came a shepherd and a shepherdess, he in a cocked hat and knee breeches and she in a short pink skirt. They bowed to each other, then retreated back into the clock. I was charmed.

"Junius . . . !" Rosalie whispered insistently.

We left.

From then on I often imagined a younger Mrs. Hammond in a blue gown with ruffles and lace, bejeweled and radiant, flicking her black lace fan as she received a procession of notables in a parlor aglow with gaslight, waving them toward a table with decanters of port and sherry, and platters of cakes and scones. I could almost hear her gown's rustle, the clink of glasses, the murmur of their talk. Then I imagined myself, regal and swank in a dark coat over a plaid vest and a ruffled white shirt, weighted with gold studs and a watch fob, inviting troops of guests toward a candle-lit dining table gleaming with china and crystal.

One morning when Mrs. Hammond lingered upstairs, I sat in her sitting-room armchair and gestured an imagined Reverend Dr. Blythe to a seat, so he could tell me how he had surprised the choir's best soprano being fondled by a vestryman: an account I would hear with glee.

"Well, well, look who's playing lord of the manor!"

When Rosalie's voice broke in, I started, leaped from the chair. As she began wielding her feather duster with a smirk, I slunk off to my slop jars and grates.

For weeks afterward, in nightly fantasies I hunted a giggling Rosalie among the shrouded shapes in the parlor, chased her around Mounted Amazon Attacked by a Tiger, spanked her on the ottoman, then rolled naked with her on the thick floral carpeting, initiating, amid smells of black walnut and plush and brocade, the most brazen acts of lechery. This rapture continued in full sight of the scandalized portraits and the open Bible. Then, just as the mantel clock chimed, and the shepherd and shepherdess jiggled out and bowed, I shot into her, and into the hint of death all around us, a joyous blast of sperm. Needless to say, a real blast accompanied this illusion, albeit self-induced, in my bed with straw ticking, in my rugless room.

Meanwhile the real Rosalie, enticing and mocking, still eluded me.

# 8

THE SLAVERY ISSUE HAD LONG BEEN COMING TO A head. When John Brown was hanged for trying to start a slave uprising in Virginia, and most of the North denounced him, I heard black people praise him and talk about the "right of rebellion." Then Lincoln got elected, the Southern states seceded, Fort Sumter was fired on, and the President called for volunteers. The feel of the town changed overnight: patriotic rallies, flags and recruiters everywhere, tents and sentinels at the Battery, and a barracks in City Hall Park. War at last with the South! I was minded to enlist.

"You can't!" said Poppa. "They ain't lettin' blacks enlist. This war ain't bein' fought for us, Junius; it's to preserve the Union. A white folks' war, so let the white folks fight."

"But Poppa, won't the slaves be freed?"

"Maybe, maybe not. Slavery's in this country's blood and bone."

"But we're in a free state, Poppa. There aren't any slaves up here."

"The slaves are all down South, Junius, but the money's up here. Who's always made loans, so the big planters could buy more land and slaves? New York City banks. Who builds the slave ships, and who makes the chains and shackles they need to keep slaves from runnin' away? Shipbuilders and iron manufactories up North, that's who!"

"But Poppa, the slave trade was abolished long ago."

"People with money can always get round the law. Slave ships bound for Africa have sailed right out of the port of New York, even as late as last year, to get slaves and sell 'em in Cuba. People will do anything for money."

"They sailed from here, Poppa?"

"Yes, Junius, they sailed from here."

I was stunned. "Poppa, how do you know all this?"

"White folks talk among themselves as if a black man wasn't even there. If a barber keeps his mouth shut and his ears open, he can learn a lot. Back when I was snippin' the white muckamucks, I heard things you wouldn't believe."

For all his scanty education, Poppa was just about the smartest black man in the city.

"And so, Junius," he concluded, "forget about enlistin'. Right now the best way you can help your people is to have a good job that gives you self-respect. This Miz Hammond don't sound so bad. She's comin' down in the world and you're movin' up. Help her any way you can. It'll all pay off in the end."

So, I stuck to my job. But with all those uniforms around, I felt out of it.

❧

So did Lester Hicks, whom I met by chance on the street, and who voiced indignation at not being allowed to fight for his brothers in the South. He was wearing a blue flannel shirt and denims, and a battered wide-brimmed hat, and looked tattered and worn.

"Junius, I was lured out to the Colorado goldfields by the promise of a mother lode of gold and went digging in a place called Treasure Hill, later renamed Last Chance Gulch. So, what did I find? Dirt. And rattlesnakes. And dust. Drought in summer, with hordes of grasshoppers that darkened the sky, stripped trees, crawled inside your pant legs, ate shovel handles right out of your hand. Blizzardy winters. To get through them, I gobbled ham hard as mahogany, gristled crows, and rats—yes, Junius: rats! I survived by gathering buffalo bones and selling them to be shipped to fertilizer plants back East. The nearest town was a suburb of hell, with drunks, thugs, outlaws, and the skinniest, meanest whores you ever saw. A murder a day. Finally I got a job as pitchman with a traveling medicine show, sold Kickapoo Wizard Oil and Pawnee Jack's Bitters to the locals—awful stuff. Well, I'm back, thank God. I was thinking of opening a gambling parlor in the Five Points, if I can scrape up the cash, and keep shy of the husband of a ladylove. But maybe this is it, really it. I'm tired, played out, bust."

I wished him luck with his new venture, but no, I wouldn't lend him three dollars.

Mrs. Hammond put a framed photograph of the President on her rosewood desk in the sitting room. Every day she had me go out to fetch a paper, preferably the *Times* or *Tribune*. Sometimes I found a newsboy shouting headlines on

Seventeenth Street; sometimes I had to walk to Sixth Avenue. When she got the paper, she hunched over it with her eyeglasses—ordinary metal-rimmed glasses, not the lorgnette she used when she wanted to look at folks with disdain. As she read, she smiled or frowned or gasped. As the war dragged on, the smiles were mighty few.

"Junius, this is a frightful struggle!"

"Junius, the news is appalling!"

"Junius, I don't know when this slaughter will end."

When she was done with the paper, she left it on her desk for me to take and read.

"You are privileged to read, Junius. By all means keep abreast of events."

I did. Besides the war news, I noticed the announcements of contracts to provide provisions and equipment to the military, and the ads for fine carriages and imported cashmere shawls, and for housemen and coachmen and grooms. Which put me in mind of something my father had said, echoing rumors he had heard in his barbershop:

"Junius, someone's gettin' rich off this war!"

On Thursdays, if the weather permitted, I would borrow my father's gig—not the one of his youthful promenades, but a new one acquired more recently—so as to gad about and get the feel of the town. Usually I confined myself to Broadway and its side streets, but one day I drove far up the Fifth Avenue, now called the axis of elegance, eyeing the fancy brownstones being built there—far more grandiose than the one I lived in—and on into the new Central Park.

I was amazed at all the greenery, at ponds and lakes shimmering in the sunlight, and at shady groves. And amazed at the parade of carriages on the Drive—phaetons, victorias, and caleches (Poppa had taught me the names), as well as ones I didn't know—driven by liveried coachmen, and attended by top-hatted grooms perched high in rumble seats, arms folded. In the carriages rode silk-hatted gentlemen in velvet coats and varnished black boots, and ladies in lace mantles and fancy silks, with parasols and bonnets.

"Shoddy!" Mrs. Hammond proclaimed them, having received reports from her minister and lawyer and the papers, thus condemning a multitude of war contractors, gold speculators, and stockbrokers and their wives. These "shoddy people" were the ones putting up those fancy new brownstones on the Avenue; Mrs. Hammond dismissed them with all the scorn that New Money inspired in the Old. I scorned them, too, glad to be living in a brownstone of quiet taste, however subdued in atmosphere and pinched for funds.

On this and subsequent excursions up the Fifth Avenue and into the Park, I was the only black man in sight not in livery; I got quite a few looks.

Mrs. Simmons and Rosalie took little interest in events, seemed to think their lives unaffected. Often as not, at our meals together Mrs. Simmons complained of the misery in her joints.

"Try rhododendron oil," I finally suggested.

Her eyes fixed me sharp. "What do you know about it?"

"Not much. But that's what Momma often uses. She's a healer."

"Your momma cures folks?"

"Often, not always. She has the Power."

Mrs. Simmons and Rosalie both gave a look.

"Could she fix me up with somethin'?" Mrs. Simmons asked. "Rhododendron oil or whatever?"

"I'll ask her."

"How does she like to be paid?"

"Anyway you can. She never worries folks for money."

"Then she really is a healer. They do it 'cause they're called to it, not 'cause they're hot after money."

So, I consulted Momma, who asked Mrs. Simmons's age and what she was like, then fixed up a mix of oils to be taken a tablespoon every three hours. Mrs. Simmons tried it and a week later gave me a report.

"Junius, your momma's a wonder. That stuff healed me good."

"Momma says the aches may come back. If they do, she'll fix you up some more."

"Now how can I pay her? I ain't got any cash."

"Your gingersnaps are wondrous good."

So, Mrs. Simmons baked two dozen gingersnaps and I took them to Momma, who sampled them and agreed that they were wondrous good.

A week later Mrs. Hammond summoned me to the sitting room, where she sat rubbing an arm.

"Junius, Mrs. Simmons says that your mother's nostrum has cleared up most of her aches."

"Yes ma'am."

"I have aches, too, as you know. Dr. Bowers is useless. Of course there's no question of my going to your mother, or of her coming to me."

At this, two thoughts hit. First: *If you won't meet Momma, why should she bother with you?* Second: *I know you don't mean to be nasty. You're locked into who and what you are, just like us. We didn't any of us plan it.* So, I said, "No ma'am."

"Could you—would you—be able to bring me that nostrum?"

"Yes ma'am."

"It would be a blessing. But what will I tell Dr. Bowers?"

"He doesn't have to know, now does he?"

"Hmm . . . No, I suppose not. So be it. Please see what your mother can do."

I was quite aware that Mrs. Hammond thought she was venturing into some kind of black magic or voodoo.

A week later I gave her a small green bottle labeled (in Cissy's hand, since Momma couldn't write) "For Mrs. Hammond's misery." She removed the stopper, sniffed it, and winced.

"It smells absolutely foul!"

"Yes ma'am."

I almost smiled. Momma always made her remedies smell foul. The worse they smelled, the more folks thought they worked.

"What is in it?"

"Momma wouldn't say. She says it's better if you don't know. But she fixed it specially for you."

"Hmm . . . Well, I'll try it."

She took a teaspoon, filled it, eyed the yellowish liquid, swallowed it, and shuddered.

"It tastes even worse than it smells!"

"Yes ma'am. Now take two more spoonfuls."

"Two more?"

"A tablespoon every three hours."

She sighed. "What people will do in desperation!"

I watched as she took two more, remembering myself and Cissy, when Momma used to feed us castor oil.

A week later she was radiant.

"Junius, I am amazingly improved. I'm converted, I've become a believer!"

"I'm so glad, ma'am. Momma's remedies usually work."

"But how can I pay her? Things are very dear these days. I have so little cash."

Since the war began, prices had soared. Her lawyer had called again, and Mr. Whipple had been summoned to cart off a handsome dresser from an empty bedroom on my floor.

"Just anything will do. Or nothing at all, if you're strapped."

"Not to pay her would be unforgivable. Here, give her this."

She held out her black-lace fan.

"Ma'am, I can't take that. It's precious."

"I have others. Please give it to her. It expresses my gratitude."

So, I took it and gave it to Momma, who was overjoyed.

"Look at that, Junius!" She flicked it open and shut again. "I ain't never had a fan like that! Wait till Bessie and Dilly see it, they'll burst with envy. It's just scrumptiously fine!"

For days to come, she flicked it at every opportunity.

❧

Rosalie had witnessed these doings in wide-eyed silence. I hoped that having a mother for a healer might hike me up in her esteem. Lately she hadn't been herself—no smirk, no teasing, just long stretches of silence; something was on her mind. One night, going up to my room, I thought I heard sobbing behind her door. I knocked gently. The sobbing stopped; no answer. I shrugged, walked away. But the next night, in my room, I heard a tapping on my door, and there she was, all wrapped up in worry.

"Junius, I've got to talk to you."

Surprised, I waved her in and closed the door. She sat on the only chair; I sat on the bed.

"Junius, I've got myself into a condition. I don't know what to do!"

It was Cissy all over again: another smarty brought down.

"Your beau won't marry you?"

"No! And even if he did, I couldn't stay on here. Mrs. Hammond wouldn't want a brat in the house. It's a good job. I need it!"

She broke down in sobs. Here she was at last in my room, elusive Rosalie, queen of my dreams, humbled and at my mercy. Yet I felt not a spark of desire, only pity.

"What do you want me to do?"

She calmed herself. "I thought maybe your mother . . ."

"Momma births babies, she doesn't kill them."

"But midwives know about these things—they must. Please ask her! Please!"

"How far along are you?"

"A month, maybe more."

"All right, I'll see what I can do."

"Oh thank you, Junius, thank you. I feel so ashamed!"

She was all but falling at my feet; it embarrassed me. I sent her to her room to get some sleep.

"Junius, I be birthin' babies, not killin' 'em!" Momma's answer was just what I expected.

"Please, Momma. She's desperate."

"I hardly almost never done it. It don't seem right!"

"She'll lose her job, Momma. She might try something foolish on her own. Please."

"How far gone is she, anyway?"

"A month or more."

"It don't seem right."

The next day I gave Rosalie a small brown flask, unlabeled.

"Take a tablespoon of this every hour, till it's gone. If it works, it'll happen in three days."

She nodded, took the flask.

Three days later Rosalie told Mrs. Hammond early in the morning that she was feeling poorly, needed to keep to her bed. I helped Mrs. Hammond downstairs and all day answered the silver bell when it rang. Toward evening I managed to tap lightly on Rosalie's door. She opened it, looked wasted.

"I got through it," she whispered. "It was ugly. I need to rest."

I nodded; she shut the door.

Since the servants' rooms had no running water and therefore no commode, I assumed that Rosalie had got rid of the evidence by emptying her slop jar into the commode in Mrs. Hammond's bathroom, whose fancy appointments—porcelain commode, marble washstand, and metal tub encased in mahogany—I had rarely seen. Fortunately, Mrs. Hammond remained downstairs till night.

Rosalie resumed her duties the next day, but she was changed. The Rosalie of the mocking smile who had teased and scolded and eluded me was gone, maybe forever; I missed her. The new Rosalie, subdued and vulnerable, could at best be only a friend.

Over time, I would begin to see the change in Rosalie as a blessing. My lust for her only served as a distraction from my real obsession. I needed to possess a brownstone and I couldn't let Rosalie or anything else get in the way of that.

# 9

BY THE SECOND YEAR OF THE WAR THERE WERE FEWER flags and rallies, and when a regiment marched off to the front, instead of cheering crowds there were only a few idlers watching. The city had got used to the war.

One day Mrs. Hammond called me into the sitting room, where she was reading the paper. She seemed excited.

"Junius, the President has issued a proclamation freeing the slaves in the South as of January 1 next. He hasn't freed all the slaves everywhere, but that will come in time. This is a very great day for your people."

I was stunned. "Glory!" was all I could say.

"My late husband was an importer. When he wasn't thinking about trade—and he thought about it much too often—he was of the opinion that all slaves should be freed. Given the temper of the times, he kept this to himself. Now, everything has changed."

When she was done with the paper, I read and reread the article; it was true. Hearing the news, Rosalie exclaimed

"High time!" and Mrs. Simmons said she had prayed for it. My family and all the black people I knew were elated.

"It's Beulah land!" said Bessie.

"It's kingdom come!" said Dilly.

Poppa and Momma hugged each other in tears.

When the freedom date came, and the city's black population held a great jubilee at the Cooper Institute, Mrs. Hammond gave me the evening off so I could go. Poppa and many of his patrons were there, including the city's black gentry, who usually kept aloof from the rest of us, considering us more or less riffraff. It was a real hodgepodge of folks, with ministers rubbing elbows with bootblacks, and teachers and restaurant owners with dishwashers and peddlers and cartmen, including the ones who carted off the tubs from the privies. We heard speeches and sang and cheered and cried "Glory!" as if the New Jerusalem had come.

In the jubilee crowd I was amazed to meet Lester Hicks in a clerical collar, neatly sideburned and sporting a flashy gold watch fob. He showed me his card, announcing the Reverend Lester Odysseus Hicks of the New Joy Zion Church, and then, looking fearfully pious, asked me if I had been washed in the blood of the Lamb. Not lately, I had to admit.

"Junius, I've found myself at last. The old Lester is a thing of the past. I've been raised up of God to do a wonderful work. I've been to the high places, I've heard the whispering of the Everlasting Covenant."

"Really? What does it say?"

"Love! Junius, I brim with benevolence. I love rocks and clouds: God's work. And people, too: God's work. And you, Junius. Scoffer though you are, I love you."

"God's work?"

"Indeed you are! For the sake of your immortal soul, please come to my church."

"I work on Sundays. My day off is Thursday."

"Ah, how Providence disposes! We have a prayer meeting on Thursday evenings to give thanks to the Bountiful Giver."

"I'm not much of a one for prayer meetings."

"Heavenly mindedness is within reach of all. Come! It will change your life."

Lester Hicks a man of the Gospel? I was skeptical, but my worst fear was that he just might be sincere. Well, for once I could check him out.

That Thursday at the New Joy Zion Church—a ramshackle frame structure on the West Side over near the river—I found a flock of pious ladies, among them my two aunts, whom this charmer had lured away from the Greater New Tabernacle Baptist Church. They greeted me with warmth.

"Oh Junius, he got the Word!" said Bessie.

"He preach up a storm!" added Dilly. "Talk like a prophet, make you see chariots of fire!"

He did. Mounting to the pulpit in a spotless robe of black velvet, he gave forth in resonant tones.

"Oh brother and sisters, flee the wrath to come! On the Day of Judgment there will be black rivers of pitch and orange torrents of brimstone sweeping away the hovels and mansions of sinners, and hurling frock-coated gentlemen and fancy ladies with parasols into the hot bonfire of hell. O what a sizzle of flesh, what a hiss and crackle of bones! Can you see them? I can. I can even smell and taste them, those vile sinners cooking in the wrath of the Lord. A stink like tainted cheese, like calves' brain gone bad, like garbage in a swamp, like privies. A taste like crab apples, like cod-liver oil, like kerosene, like soap. Smells and tastes to make you puke and spit!"

By now, all around me ladies were weeping and moaning. Lester's oratory, accompanied by sweeping gestures, had sent shivers down my spine, roiled my stomach, and brought my lips to a pucker.

"But look"—as he pointed toward the rafters and beyond, his voice became soaring and lyrical—"look up there in heaven: the dear saved saints, the white-robed troops of glory, are being chorused by angels into heaven! O the shining robes, the sweet scent of lilac and camphor, the rippling music of harps, the joyous going home! O my friends, to be in the ranks of the saved! O it is honey, it is roses, it is balm of Gilead. It is like being bathed in clean water or kissed by the morning dew."

"Amen!" and "Yeah, brother!" came the cries around me. Was I imagining it? I smelled lilac and camphor, and felt like I'd just had a bath.

Lester's eyes were blazing, his voice was passionate.

"O to say, 'I have seen the Presence, I have heard the Word!' O may the Spirit enter me and force and lift and gladden me, and boost me toward the heights! O mene mene tekel upharsin! O shadrach meshach abednego! O poobah pelethite! Assir zadok himmel ahitub! Iggly ithamar! Issachar boobly amminadab! Naphtali! Amiga! Naphtali!"

What was happening? He was mouthing gibberish, a cross between baby talk and the foreign languages I had heard snatches of on the streets, with a Biblical touch thrown in. The ladies, eyes shut, tearing, were listening with rapt attention. Then it hit: he was speaking in tongues, or giving a first-rate imitation of it. I was dumbfounded. Lester Hicks, speaking in tongues!

Then he came out of it and, not missing a beat, launched into the offertory:

"Give, brother and sisters, that we may build a house of worship worthy of this congregation." (Cries of "Yes, brother, yes!")

"Give, that we may wash away our sins, be reborn, know the kiss of brotherhood, and rise into the Light!" (Cries of "Bet your boots!" and "Yes sirree!")

"Give, that we may walk in green valleys and drink the Sweet Waters of Truth, that we may climb the Mount of Righteousness, and with the brick of our prayer and the mortar of our song build the New Zion Church of Joy!" (Cries of "Halleloo!" and "Glory!")

Into the offering bowl, when it was passed around, went a shower of greenbacks and coins, several knobbed silver pins, a gold buckle, and at least one rhinestone. Even I parted with a buck. I was impressed. Lester had found himself at last.

The colored people had celebrated emancipation, but the feel of the town was different. Stories circulated of black stevedores being attacked on the docks by striking white laborers who said, "The niggers take our jobs!" Then the government imposed a draft, but let rich folks escape it by paying three hundred dollars for a substitute. When I drove out in Poppa's gig, I got more looks than ever, boys cried "Nigger!" and someone threw a rock. By summer I stopped driving. There was feeling against the draft, the rich, and the blacks. Nobody was shouting "Glory!" now.

On a Friday in July, soon after news of the victories at Vicksburg and Gettysburg, the draft began in New York; according to the Saturday papers, it went well. All weekend the weather was sticky and hot. Mrs. Hammond sipped iced syrups and fanned herself with a big straw fan. At night I slept naked, sweating in my upstairs room. On Monday morning fire bells clanged in the distance, there was running in the street. I went up to the third floor and looked out a window facing north. Here and there above the roofs, dark smoke was rising, some wispy and thin, some thick and billowing; there was a burnt smell in the air.

When I informed Mrs. Hammond in the sitting room, she frowned, pursed her lips.

"There must be a disturbance. You will not go out today on errands. I will dine at one as usual."

That afternoon she sat hunched over her ledgers at the desk, seemingly unconcerned, then had supper and retired at ten. In my stuffy room at the top of the house, I heard fire bells clanging off and on all night, and shouts and gunshots. I scarcely slept.

The next morning, hearing a newsboy screaming headlines in the street, I darted out to get a paper. "Nigger, get off the street!" cried the boy, less as a threat than a warning. Puzzled, I glanced at the headlines:

**RIOT**
**BUILDINGS FIRED**
**SOLDIERS MOBBED**
**BROWNSTONES SACKED**

I rushed back inside, thrust the paper at Mrs. Hammond in the sitting room. She devoured it, tense with alarm.

"Junius," she announced, "the draft office has been burned, policemen assaulted, the Colored Orphan Asylum destroyed, the mayor's home attacked. Brownstones have been pillaged, and colored men lynched in the street. The police are outnumbered. Until troops return from Gettysburg, Irish mobs rule the city!"

Our eyes met; we read each other's fear. The very worst that could happen was happening.

"I've got to go to my family!"

"No! I forbid you to leave this house! You would never reach your family. You would be maimed or killed in the street. Stay here where you're needed. You're the only man on the premises."

I knew that she was right. For the moment, my family were on their own.

"Junius, what shall we do?"

It was an appeal; all that she had was at risk.

"Call the others. We've got to stay cool, plan, and defend ourselves." But my brain was whirling.

With her bell she summoned Rosalie, who fetched Mrs. Simmons from the kitchen.

"There is an insurrection in the city," she announced. "Irish mobs are running wild. Colored people have been assaulted, brownstones burned. No decent person is safe on the streets." She paused a moment, to let this news sink in. "Junius will advise us what to do."

Three pairs of frightened eyes looked to me. I felt a cold calm; power was mine.

"We mustn't any of us leave this house, or even show ourselves at windows where we can be seen from the street. Rosalie and I will close the upstairs shutters and barricade both front doors, and fill all the bathtubs with water. Mrs. Simmons, heat up a lot of water on the stove and keep it boiling hot. And fill all the pails you can with cold water. The cold water's for putting out fires; the hot water's for rioters. Mrs. Hammond, are there any guns in the house?"

"My husband's revolver."

"Give it me. And the two sturdiest knives from the kitchen. I'll guard the doors. If anyone tries to force his way in, he'll get a scalded face, a stab, and a bump on the head. And if that's not enough, a bullet. No one's going to burn this brownstone!"

"Why would they want to?" stammered Rosalie.

"They might think someone lives here connected with the draft. Or that we're sheltering a wounded policeman. Or that black people live and work here. Or that it looks too rich and fancy."

Rosalie started whimpering; I slapped her.

"Stop it! Stay calm!"

"Lord preserve us!" exclaimed Mrs. Simmons, who was praying already.

"You have your instructions," said Mrs. Hammond. "Report to Junius when you are done. I will remain here in the sitting room and will dine at one as usual."

While Mrs. Simmons returned to the kitchen to set water a-boil on the stove, Rosalie and I shuttered all the front windows on the floors above, then moved a heavy chest against the front door, and an old trunk against the door in the basement, and filled the tubs with water. Once Rosalie had brought me the revolver and two long knives from the kitchen, I found a sturdy stick in a wood box in the cellar and tested it by striking it on the flagstones of the cellar floor. By the time I was done, I had quite an arsenal assembled in the front hall near the door. I tried to look calm, but now my hands were trembling.

All morning it was quiet outside. When Mrs. Hammond dined at one, I served her in silence, as if nothing were amiss. That afternoon I kept watch at an upstairs window, peeking out to see more smoke rising from different parts of the city. Rosalie was making a pretense of dusting, checking with me every few minutes, while Mrs. Simmons read her Bible in the kitchen, and Mrs. Hammond leafed through albums at her desk. Amazingly, I was in charge, ready to defend this brownstone as my own. "Grab the power," Poppa had told me; power had dropped in my lap.

That night there were shouts and scurryings in the street. Spreading a blanket in the hall by the front door, I dozed, woke up, dozed, woke up, then finally drifted into sleep. In my dreams fire consumed drapes and upholstery, bric-a-brac kindled, carpeting flamed, and as the whole house smoked and crackled, huge chandeliers plummeted and crashed on the floor. I woke up in a sweat, looked around me; all was quiet.

The next morning, hearing another newsboy shouting, I darted out, got a paper, darted back.

## THE REIGN OF THE RABBLE
## DWELLINGS PLUNDERED
## MORE NEGROES HUNG

The whole city was paralyzed, an armory had been looted, and a black cartman beaten to death, his corpse hung from a tree and set aflame, while rioters yelled and danced beneath it. Reading of black refugees fleeing the city on steamboats, some of them penniless and begging the fare, I wondered if my family had joined the exodus or, worse still, had been attacked. So, this was freedom!

"I will dine at one as usual," Mrs. Hammond announced.

All afternoon I kept watch at an upstairs window, peeking out. Men and boys ran by, and fire bells clanged again in the distance. Late that night, on guard behind the barricaded front door, I heard more shouts and running in the street, then steps coming up the stoop. Suddenly there flashed in my mind the image of the Irish butcher boy who long ago had sicced his dog on me and laughed as I ran in terror. We blacks had run too much; this time I would fight.

The revolver in one hand and a knife in the other, I waited. More steps on the stoop, murmurs of talk; I tensed. Silence: time seemed suspended; my fingers tightened on the revolver and knife. Then, quietly, the steps retreated. More shouts erupted in the distance, faded away. I breathed again, but slept in the hall all night.

On Thursday, the fourth day of the riots, it was strangely calm outside. Peering again from an upstairs window, I saw smoke from fewer fires, heard distant cheering, a sound of drums and marching: the troops had returned from

Gettysburg! Later I went out, bought several papers, saw shops opening on Sixth Avenue, and horsecars running; the riots seemed to have stopped.

"Please, Mrs. Hammond, I've got to go to my family!"

"Of course you do. Run!"

Slipping the loaded revolver in my shirtfront, I hurried out. Going down Sixth Avenue with no soldiers or police in sight, I ducked into doorways or side streets whenever I saw what might be a gang of toughs up ahead. There were no burnt buildings in the area, but smears of ash from bonfires, and smack in the middle of the street, a smashed pianoforte. Its black and white keys were scattered, and its innards exposed; men and boys were breaking it up for fuel. Occasionally a shot rang out in the distance.

Suddenly I heard the cry of "Nigger!" and saw a bunch of men and boys rushing toward me. Dashing into a side street, I scaled a fence, crossed an empty back yard, scaled another fence, startled a woman watering her garden, scaled a third fence. Behind me the cries of "Nigger!" still rang out; they were after me, just one fence away. Scaling a fourth fence wore me out. Turning, I whipped out the revolver, waited. I heard shouts and footsteps. Two hands grasped the top of the fence. Then, hoisting himself up, a burly man in a slouch hat appeared, with a swarthy face, and a knife clenched in his teeth. Seeing me point the revolver at him, he looked surprised; I fired. He shrieked, fell back; his comrades screamed and cursed. Quickly I scaled the next fence, found myself in a narrow alleyway that led to a street. There were no more shouts behind me.

It had all happened so fast, I had had no time to think. Had I killed a man? I didn't know. Had I even hit him? I wasn't sure.

I'd never fired a gun before, knew nothing about them. All I knew was that, when I fired, he'd fallen back in the other yard. Slipping the revolver in my shirtfront, I hurried on, looking warily about. Until I reached Minetta Lane, not one black person did I see; all had fled or were in hiding.

On Minetta Lane I found the whole block untouched, my family in turmoil. Bessie was hollering and praying, Dilly weeping, Cissy shushing them, the baby wailing, Momma mixing something to calm them, and Poppa sitting off in a corner, dazed. Seeing me, they hugged and kissed me, laughed, cried, praised the Lord. After the quiet of the brownstone, a hullabaloo and hubbub of love.

Neither his house nor his barbershop had been damaged, and the whole family was safe, but Poppa just sat in his chair, hands trembling, shaking his head.

"In all the years I been in this city, I ain't never seen nothin' like this."

He'd heard about black boardinghouses being gutted, to cries of "Burn down the cribs of the niggers!" And a black man lynched, his whole body gashed, his fingers and toes sliced off. There were stories of Irish bullies boasting of having "done for a nigger," and black families sleeping overnight in station houses, and black corpses so beaten to jelly that they couldn't be identified at the morgue.

"Never seen nothin' like this," he kept saying. "Never seen such hate."

"It's awful, Poppa," I said, "but the troops have arrived. It's over."

But he just kept shaking his head. Though they were all safe, I left with a heavy heart.

❧

"Junius, you may return those knives to the kitchen and give me the revolver. Rosalie has opened the upstairs shutters. I will dine at one."

With this announcement on the day after my visit to Minetta Lane, power slipped from me; the brownstone returned to normal.

"Junius," said Mrs. Hammond, "you were a rock of granite. Words cannot express my gratitude."

The granite rock was soon raking out the furnace, cleaning coal grates, toting slop jars and trash. No one noticed that a bullet was missing; I said nothing.

❧

On my next Thursday off, with a sheathed knife in my shirt, I poked about on foot, viewing the charred timbers, bricks, and rubble of what had once been shabby colored boardinghouses. Here and there loomed burnt hulks of white-owned brownstones as well, windows smashed, innards stripped and gutted, stoop and street littered with broken glass and chinaware, scraps of scorched wood, shreds of velvet and brocade. And I had thought brownstones, with their thick walls and steep stoop, safe!

And was I myself safe on the streets? Things were quiet now, but for how long? In dreams for weeks to come I saw a swarthy face climbing a fence with a knife clenched in its teeth, heard a shot, saw the face disappear. Even in the North, for killing a white man blacks had been hanged, whipped to death, burnt alive, mutilated. Was I a killer? The newspapers had told me nothing. I would never know.

In the weeks and months that followed the riots, whenever I saw my family on Minetta Lane, Poppa was always sitting in his chair, shaking his head, staring, muttering. Some of his friends had fled to the woods north of the city, or to the sandy barrens of Long Island, or to the hills and swamps of New Jersey, but came back; others had vanished forever. Even the black elite had had to flee, and some of them, returning, found no home, only burnt bricks and ash. No matter how rich and respectable, no black person had been safe. Mulling all this over day after day, Poppa stopped going to the barbershop, and let his two assistants handle such patrons as dared come in.

"Somethin' in him is broke," said Momma. "Somethin' I can't fix."

When I tried to talk to him, he just stared straight ahead, barely acknowledged me, never looked me in the eye. "Never seen such hate," he kept saying over and over again. Though he hadn't seen it, the violence of the riots was stamped on his brain forever.

**MEN OF COLOR**
**TO ARMS! TO ARMS!**
**NOW OR NEVER**
**FAIL NOW, & OUR RACE IS DOOMED**

Going out on my day off, I saw the posters all over town. Blacks were finally being allowed, even encouraged, to enlist, and black regiments were already marching off to war, cheered by blacks and whites alike. What was I doing in a brownstone? Feverish, I rushed back and told Mrs. Hammond that

I was giving her one month's notice.

"You must not leave me, Junius!" she protested. "You are needed here."

"Mrs. Hammond, I want to help my people down there. I want to fight against the slaveholding South!"

"That is admirable, Junius, but I need you here. There are others who can fight."

"Ma'am, I've got to do it."

"Do you want more money, Junius? You know I'm short of cash."

"It's not a question of money, Mrs. Hammond."

"Then what *is* it a question of?"

"Dignity. The government has finally recognized our worth."

"I see. I respect that, Junius. They need you, and I need you. Well, here's what I propose. Stay with me another six months. If, at the end of that time, this awful war is still raging, I'll let you go and even wish you well."

"Six months is a long time, Mrs. Hammond. Let's make it three."

"No, six months, I beg of you. Don't leave me before that. I need you, Junius. Please stay!"

There was a hint of desperation in her voice; it surprised me.

"All right, ma'am, six months to the day."

I marked the date in my calendar and with heavy heart stayed on. As the battlefront news got better, everyone but me rejoiced and hoped for a speedy end to the war.

When I consulted Poppa about enlisting, he gave me a blank stare. "Do what you think best." He was still depressed.

One week before Grant captured Richmond, Poppa died in his sleep. "Heart failure," said the doctor. "Heart ache," said Momma. Bessie and Dilly argued for a service by the Reverend Lester at the New Joy Zion Church, which had survived the riots and was flourishing.

"He's so good at funerals," said Bessie.

"Speak so soft and soothin'," said Dilly. "Make everybody cry."

But Momma insisted on the Greater New Tabernacle Baptist Church, which Poppa had occasionally attended. There, Bessie and Dilly hollered their grief and Cissy wept, while Momma and I sat silent, holding hands. It was good that I was there. Another strong woman, Momma, needed me.

"That man been so good to me, Junius," she told me later. "Been good to me past tellin'."

The gig was mine; I had no heart to use it. Like Momma, I couldn't find the words to express my feeling for this quiet, loving man who had known his limitations and accepted them; who was respectful of others and slow to judge them; who loathed violence and brutality; who worked quietly to help his people; who was there when I needed him, but let me do my growing. More than anything, I missed his cagey wisdom.

When, just before my six months with Mrs. Hammond were up, Richmond fell and everyone knew the war was over, and Rosalie laughed and Mrs. Simmons sang, and Mrs. Hammond had an extra glass of sherry at lunch, I could only half celebrate. And when the President was killed a few days later, and Rosalie and Mrs. Simmons wept, and Mrs. Hammond wore a black band of mourning, and inked his photograph on her desk with an X, I could only half grieve, since I had grieving of my own to finish. Even my regret at not having enlisted I managed to forget for a while. I all but sleepwalked through those joyful and calamitous times.

# 10

DURING THE MONTHS FOLLOWING THE WAR'S END I heard rapturous accounts from Bessie and Dilly about the Reverend Lester's oratory, and the building plans of the New Joy Zion Church, which were about to be realized at last. Lester, that perennial adventurer, seemed to have finally found his niche in the pulpit. But then my aunts reported some doubts and dissension festering in the midst of the flock, mostly concerning financial matters that they knew little about.

Then, one Thursday when I was visiting my family, my aunts were on hand to report that the Reverend Lester Odysseus Hicks had absconded.

"That man sweet-talked us out of our savings," Dilly said, in tears.

I was stunned. "He cheated you pure and simple?"

"Nothin' pure about it," said Dilly. "Someone asked for somethin' called an audit, and he just whooshed away. He's gone and so is our money. All we got left is that crumbly old buildin' about to fall down on our heads."

"Junius," said Bessie, "if your path ever crosses his again, please direct him our way, so we can spike his guts on hatpins and scalp his holy noggin with a cleaver. Right now we just ain't feelin' too Christian."

Chagrinned, they reverted to the Greater New Tabernacle Baptist Church. For months to come, I saw no sign of Lester. Remembering the Paradigms of Vice and Virtue that Mr. Walsh had so dinned into us at school—echoes of which I had discerned in Lester's preaching—I decided that the Reverend Lester Odysseus Hicks must be wandering somewhere near the hovels of Lying and Cheating, not far from the State Prison with its corpse-dangling gallows, well on the way to hell.

Mrs. Hammond was now staying in her room more often. When, helped by Rosalie, she did come downstairs, she came slowly, clutching the banister, measuring every step. Once seated, though, she seemed very much herself.

She was in steady correspondence with her lawyer, Mr. Webb. One afternoon he called, a clean-shaven man with fluffy sideburns, accompanied by two young clerks. They were closeted with her in the sitting room for over an hour. As I went about my tasks in the house, at intervals I heard raised voices.

"But it's unheard of!" protested Mr. Webb.

"Well, it's heard of now, because I'm doing it!" Mrs. Hammond proclaimed defiantly.

Later, while Mr. Webb lingered with her, and I was giving the clerks their hats in the hall, I heard their comments.

"Cantankerous old thing, isn't she?"

"But what a sense of humor!"

When Mr. Webb joined them, he had a sour look, but said nothing. They left.

❧

A year after Poppa's death, Momma for the first time ever started saying how she didn't like living in the city.

"Folks here live so crowded up, Junius. They're so cold and unspoken in their ways. No porches to sit on, no big sunny yard for plantin', just that dark little space in back. No sun, no trees, just smells."

It worried me, hearing her talk like that. Then, one Thursday when I was visiting, she announced:

"I be goin' back to the mountains."

"Momma, you can't leave me and Cissy."

"You're all right now, Junius. You be growed and you got a good job. And Cissy'll be all right, too."

"Don't leave us, Momma!"

"My time here is done. The Lord's been warnin' me to leave. He say, 'Woman, your time here be almost done. Get ready to leave.' And I don't talk back to the Lord."

My heart sank. When Momma started talking about the Lord, there was no arguing with her; her mind was made up tight.

"When'll you go, Momma?"

"When the Lord tells me to. Now don't be fractious and fuss at me, and don't tell Bessie or Dilly. I love you, Junius, but you don't need me now, and I gotta do what I gotta do."

All week I worried, but when Thursday came again and I hurried to the house, she was still there with no sign of packing.

"The Lord ain't told me yet. Now give your old momma a kiss, Junius, and I be off to Sullivan Street to bring a baby." Then she looked right at me. "Junius, in all these years no lady never up and died on me. I been all times purity clean."

And she took her bag and left.

When I came the following week, she was gone, and so were Cissy and Virginia Sweets. Their belongings were gone, too, but everything else was there. On the table in the kitchen was an envelope, and inside it a deed to the house. Momma had given the house to me, signing the deed with an X before two witnesses. The envelope had a lawyer's name and address; it all looked legal. I couldn't get over the quiet of the house, felt lonesome to death.

When I told Bessie and Dilly, they got in a stew.

"That woman run off and leave her kin?" said Bessie. "What kind of action is that?"

"She a strange one, Junius, always was," said Dilly. "Mountains, indeed! Maybe she run off with a man!"

But I knew better. I told them they could move back into the house on Minetta Lane and live there free of rent, as long as they kept a room for me, should I ever need it. Being hard up for rent where they were, they jumped at the chance.

"Junius, you so good to us!"

"We open a boardin'house. We fix that place up good!"

I knew I'd never see Momma again. She had taken Cissy and Virginia Sweets off into that mysterious world of womankind and healing that I could never enter. I had more grieving to do.

By the second year after the war, Mrs. Hammond no longer came downstairs; Rosalie attended her and took up her meals. I knew what Momma would have said: "She fixin' to die." Momma always knew when folks had got past healing. Dr. Bowers and the Reverend Blythe called, but came away shaking their heads; the reverend could no longer elicit peals of laughter.

"She's in no pain," said Rosalie. "Just feeble. And does she ever boss me around! Fetch this, do that—no end of it."

"Well, I guess it won't be long."

"Guess not."

The thought of Mrs. Hammond's passing upset me. She was a friend of sorts and, for all her moods, someone I respected. In her service I had fulfilled my dream of living in a brownstone. If she died, what would become of it and of me?

"She wants to see you," Rosalie informed me one morning.

Once again I found a shrunken old woman lost in a huge four-poster. When I saw her face, I was shocked; in just a few days she had aged.

"Junius, I have some last instructions."

"Excuse me, ma'am, but has it come to that?"

"Of course it has! Now be quiet and listen; I'll tell you only once. When I go, you will inform Dr. Bowers and my lawyer Mr. Webb, who will inform my daughter Clara in Boston. I will be laid out in the parlor, so you and Rosalie will open it up and dust. There will not be many callers. Now this is very important—are you listening?"

"Yes ma'am."

"The funeral will be planned by Isaac Brown, the sexton of Grace Church. This will annoy the Reverend Blythe immensely, but no matter. Mr. Brown will see to it with taste and elegance. My daughter is to have nothing to do with it. I doubt if she'll even attend. Please repeat that back to me."

"Your daughter is to have nothing to do with it. You doubt if she'll even attend."

"Exactly. The service will be here in the parlor; no music, and God knows, no eulogy; the Reverend Blythe can preside. I want a mahogany casket with satin lining; Mr. Brown will see to it. Then a glass-plated hearse to Green-Wood, where I shall lie beside my husband. For the monument, no winged cherubs or draped urns or other rubbish; just match my husband's stone. Can you remember all this?"

"Yes ma'am. Mrs. Hammond, I'm so sorry. I—"

"Don't be sorry! It's time I went; life here is a bore. I'm going to something different, maybe something strange and wonderful, and I intend to enjoy it, or at least take full advantage. So, go away and let an old woman get on with her dying."

I left.

Two days later Rosalie found her slumped over in bed; she had died in the night. We informed Dr. Bowers and Mr. Webb. At first, Rosalie and I had no time to mourn; we were busy opening up the shutters and drapes in the parlor, removing dustcovers, dusting, scrubbing, polishing. Gradually the old splendor returned. The chandelier glowed with gaslight, the white marble fireplace shone, candelabras and andirons gleamed, the two gilt-framed portraits looked down in majesty, and the Bible lay open on its stand to DEATHS, inviting the next inscription. Death had brought the room back to life. A sumptuous setting for a funeral; I gloried in it.

Isaac Brown of Grace Church, a ruddy-faced, paunchy man in a black tie and a snow-white shirt, came and at once took charge. With Rosalie's help he lay Mrs. Hammond out in black silk in a polished mahogany casket; she looked more natural than when I had seen her last. A few callers came, all elderly, none of whom I'd ever seen before. Several returned for the funeral, which Rosalie, Mrs. Simmons, and I attended, standing well in back; the daughter did not come. The Reverend Blythe uttered a few soothing thoughts—"Mourn her not; she is folded in gold in heaven, sleeps in sheets of glory"—and said a prayer, then four sturdy pallbearers eased the closed casket down the steep front stoop and into the hearse, attracting the neighborhood's attention. The hearse drove off; she was gone. I was teary-eyed, Rosalie was sniffing, Mrs. Simmons was blubbering. Finding the album with daguerreotypes on Mrs. Hammond's desk in the sitting room, I leafed through it till I found a portrait of her in her glory and inked it out with an X.

That was Tuesday. The will, Mr. Webb had informed us, would be read on Thursday; Miss Clara was expected on Wednesday. To my surprise, Mr. Webb said that the servants should attend the reading.

On Wednesday afternoon Clara Judd strode briskly into the hall, thrust a hat with a dotted black veil at Rosalie, and met the three of us in the sitting room. A woman of forty, she had a fine-boned face with a cold symmetry that most would take for beauty, and wore her hair swept back in fashionable waterfall curls. She nodded civilly to me and Rosalie, and when Mrs. Simmons, dewy-eyed, exclaimed, "Miss Clara, it's been ages," she extended her cheek for a kiss.

"I'm terribly tired, please show me to my room," she said, tugging off a lilac kid glove to reveal a blue-gemmed hand.

Rosalie led her up to the second-floor bedroom in back; I followed with her bandbox and valise. Almost at once she strode into her mother's bedroom, looked about; we stood at the door.

"Where are the jewels?" she demanded, having opened the large gilt box on the dresser.

"At my suggestion," I explained, "Mr. Webb took them for security. He has them in his safe." (Under the circumstances, I was afraid that Rosalie might be just a bit light-fingered.)

"Hmm . . . Appropriate, I suppose."

She retired to her room to rest.

At supper that evening she wanted port, not sherry; sent back a fork as dirty; said the soup was too salty; left much of her food untouched.

The next morning we all assembled in the parlor for Mr. Webb's reading of the will. Mrs. Judd came in last, wearing black silk adorned with tucks of crepe. She nodded to us, expressionless. She sat, we sat. Mr. Webb cleared his throat and began the reading.

"I, Amelia Hammond of West Seventeenth Street, New York City, being of sound mind and memory, do hereby make, publish, and declare this to be my last will and testament, hereby revoking any and all wills and codicils previously made by me.

"First, I direct that my executor, Mr. Cyrus Webb of the firm of Webb & Willard, New York, pay all my just debts, taxes, and funeral expenses.

"Second, I bequeath my real estate on West Seventeenth Street, including all structures thereon and all furnishings therein, with the exception of the bequests specified below, to my cousin Grace Trescott of Cleveland, Ohio."

"Third, I make the following bequests:

To Hannah Simmons, my cook, for her devoted service of many years, my black lace mantle and the sum of one thousand dollars.

To Rosalie Wood, my maidservant, for putting up with my endless quirks and whims, my topaz earrings, which I know she admires, and the sum of five hundred dollars.

To Junius Fox, my waiter, for his faithful service and his strength in time of crisis, my late husband's diamond breast pin and malacca walking stick, and the sum of five hundred dollars.

To my daughter Clara Judd of Boston, for her unswerving filial duty and affection over the years, the sum of one dollar and no cents, my best porcelain chamber pot, and my dentures, both uppers and lowers, in the hope that, when needed, they will fit her rather large mouth."

Hearing this, Rosalie tittered, and I bit my lip hard so I wouldn't. Mrs. Judd sprang to her feet, flashed a look of rage at us all, and stalked out of the room. We could hear her stomping up the hallway stairs.

Mr. Webb finished the reading straight-faced, and we all marveled: the brownstone had gone to a cousin in Cleveland none of us had ever heard of! And the three of us servants felt rich. Mr. Webb suggested that we claim the objects bequeathed us now, so he could witness and record it, though he would have to fetch the jewels from his safe. The cash bequests might have to wait, he said, until he had conferred with Grace Trescott about selling some or all of her newly inherited property. He added that Mrs. Hammond had deposited references for all of us in his office, to be available to future employers.

As we stepped into the hall, down the stairs came Mrs. Judd, bandbox and valise in hand, with not a trace of black in evidence. "You'll hear from my lawyer!" she announced, then strode out the door and slammed it; we could hear her clomping down the stoop. Mr. Webb assured us that the will was valid and properly witnessed. When we went up to claim our bequests, Rosalie noticed at once that Mrs. Judd had appropriated her mother's ivory-handled silk parasol and all her fans.

At Mr. Webb's invitation, we stayed on in the brownstone until he informed us that Grace Trescott was selling the residence and all its contents, claiming for herself only the family Bible, several albums of photographs, and the two gilt-framed portraits in the parlor. Soon after, Mr. Whipple and an army of helpers arrived with three carts and toted out all the furnishings, leaving only a few items in our bedrooms and the kitchen so we could stay one more night; he would collect them the next day. Before my very eyes I saw portraits and pianoforte lugged off, then chairs, tables, ottomans, gilt mirrors and whatnots, four-posters and other beds, bureaus, dressing tables, clocks, until all that remained was the stripped shell of the brownstone where I had lived so richly for years.

Dazed, I wandered through each of the empty rooms, assailed by a host of memories.

Mrs. Simmons went on to another job, and Rosalie to a sister's lodgings, until she could find employment. When we parted, we all shook hands, then hugged; I parted from Rosalie with some vivid memories but without desire or regret. Returning to the house on Minetta Lane, I found it so full of boarders that I had to reclaim my old dormer-windowed nook in the garret, without running water or heat. I had come full circle.

Yet I was not downhearted. When I ventured out on the street, I strutted with a diamond breast pin on my shirt-front, sporting an ivory-handled malacca walking stick with a gleaming silver collar. Black folks noticed, and those who remembered my father smiled and called me "Dandy Fox, Jr." I liked that.

I was ready to move up. Having been a waiter in a brownstone for years, I had mastered the mysteries of the hot-air furnace, coal grates, and a coal-burning stove, the ritual of genteel dining, and even—from a distance—the marvels of the shower bath and flush commode. So, now I was eager to "buttle." Even though the riots had demonstrated that the homes of the wealthy were no safer than the tenements and shanties of the poor, I still dreamed of a brownstone. But now I required a house in full glory, its parlor on display, its luxury in evidence, its residents living to the hilt. A brownstone whose vibrant life I could share in, a brownstone I could possess.

# II

# 11

"JUNIUS, AIN'T YOU NEVER GONNA FIND A JOB? YOU been interviewed for a job in three different brownstones and you turned your nose up at all of them. How come?"

"Because none of them was right, Aunt Dilly."

When the subject came up in the kitchen over meals, neither of my aunts could understand. Yes, I had listed myself for a butler's job with a black intelligence agency, and yes, I had been interviewed three times by the mistress of a brownstone. But the first lady was shabby (soiled hems, faded silks, dirty lace), the second stingy (a meager six dollars a week), and the third a scold. I would not compromise; I was aiming high.

Promenading one fine autumn afternoon on Broadway, where I loved to watch the bustle and mix of people, I encountered the Reverend Lester Odysseus Hicks, late of the New Joy Zion Church, sporting no clerical collar, but a yellow topper, check trousers, and a green frock coat over a red satin vest cut low to display a shirtfront diamond twice as big as mine. Greeting me enthusiastically, he hustled me off to a black-owned sliver of a bar down a dingy side street, where over a mug of ale he announced his newfound mission: as an agent—well, assistant agent to a subassistant commissioner—of the Freedmen's Bureau, to assist the multitudes of emancipated slaves in the South.

"Our benighted brothers and sisters need encouragement and guidance—especially to the polls on election day. We're feeding the hungry, building hospitals and hope, schools and self-respect. I fill in for the subassistant commissioner when he isn't quite sober. All in all, a most rewarding work."

So I gathered from his shirtfront diamond.

"That's all very fine, Lester, but what happened to the New Joy Zion Church?"

"A sad chapter, that. A lovely dream destroyed by false accusations, stinginess, and bickering."

"You owe two aunts of mine one hundred dollars each, the whole of their life's savings."

"All a misunderstanding that in time will be cleared up."

"Let's clear it up right now: two hundred dollars!"

To my astonishment, he took his wallet, counted out two hundred dollars in greenbacks, and gave them to me.

"Let's speak no more of that sad matter. At the time I was truly inspired, I swear I was!"

"You've come down from the heights?"

"Dragged down by traitors and the faint of heart."

"You don't brim with benevolence? You don't love rocks and clouds?"

"When I look at them now, a rock is just a rock, a cloud is just a cloud. Alas. But you know, Junius, when I spoke in tongues, I wasn't faking it."

"C'mon, Lester."

"I swear! When the mood was right, it just happened. Something took hold of me, something I couldn't control. It was thumpingly big, overwhelming. I was as surprised as anyone."

I stared into his earnest dark eyes, found no hint of duplicity. I was amazed.

"But no matter," he continued, "I've found myself again in the noble work of the Freedmen's Bureau. You might consider it yourself."

"Not likely."

"Still hankering after your brownstone, I suppose?"

"I've worked in one, I'm looking for another."

"You dream small. But I happen to know of one that needs a butler." He scribbled something on a piece of paper. "Don't mention me; I'm unknown to them. I heard of it from a friend who works there." He handed me the paper. "Here—if you must be a flunkey."

I took it and put it in my pocket. "I'm not a flunkey, Lester."

"Yes, you are. A nice little house nigger, Massa and Missy's pet."

"And you, Lester, what are you? By your own account you've been a pastry cook's helper, a merchant seaman to the land of coconuts, a prospector in Colorado, a minister of the Gospel, and now an agent for a subassistant something-or-other down South. A bit of a drifter, don't you think? My brownstone obsession anchors me."

His eyes narrowed. "Junius, while you're playing flunkey in a brownstone, I'll be out doing all the things that you dare only to dream of!"

With that, he left. I had to pay for his ale.

His words stung. I remembered Poppa cautioning me, "Junius, you may live and work in a brownstone, but you ain't never gonna own one." So, was I just a flunkey? A self-deluded domestic intruding on someone else's property? No! Mrs. Hammond's brownstone had belonged to me as well. She had been shutting it off, ignoring it, making it share in her decline. I treasured it, savored it, caressed and tasted it. In the end, it was far more mine than hers, I possessed it. And I would do it again, even more grandly. To live richly and meaningfully, amid sumptuous surroundings in an atmosphere of elegance and taste—this would fulfill me, this would be my freedom.

That evening, emptying my pockets in my bedroom, I found the scrap of paper Lester had given me, with the name Ida Clayborn and an address on East Thirty-eighth Street, a neighborhood rich in brownstones. Should I? I shrugged and went to bed.

At ten the next morning, wearing my tan frock coat, silk hat, and black satin vest, I was on East Thirty-eighth Street, studying the brownstone in question, a four-story residence with a basement and a mansard roof, one of those steep new sloping roofs, then all the rage, with projecting dormer windows. Larger than Mrs. Hammond's, but decorous in the extreme, differing in no way from the other brownstones on the block. Had I overdone it with my breast pin and walking stick? No, the neighborhood breathed elegance, demanded it. But would I really apply? After all, I had no appointment. Some blind urge drove me on.

Just then a man appeared at the top of the stoop, skittered down the steps, glanced at me on the sidewalk, hurried off. I knew that glance: just a nigger, nothing to worry about. He had looked at me as if I wasn't there. The master of the house? A gentleman, certainly, but his nervous demeanor did not proclaim him a master of property; at least, not of *this* property. A caller? Too early. Strange. I gave it up.

Going round to the basement door, I rapped the knocker, waited. And waited and waited. Finally the door was opened by a young black woman in an apron.

"Good morning, I'm Junius Fox. I'm applying for the position of butler."

She smiled. "We weren't expecting applicants till later. Come in."

The maid closed the door quietly and led me down the hallway and up a flight of stairs; no smirk, no rebuke, just movements that flowed like music. By the time we reached the parlor floor, I was comparing her poise and quiet grace to the opening of a rose, the translucence of fine china, the iridescence of mother-of-pearl. In less than two minutes she had made me a poet and a lover.

In the upstairs hallway she took my hat and walking stick, then showed me into the front parlor.

"Please have a seat. Mrs. Clayborn will be down shortly. Be patient. Morning is our quiet time. We're more alert and active in the evening."

"Thank you, miss . . ." I said, then realized I still didn't know her name.

"Thelma," she said, smiled again, and left. She had read my thought. Her soft voice lingered in my ear.

I looked about: opulence. A higher ceiling than at Mrs. Hammond's, and a longer vista. No sliding doors closed off the front parlor from the middle room; the eye was carried far into the depths of the house. Ornate moldings, elaborate crystal chandeliers, the inevitable white marble fireplace with a mantel clock backed by a huge gilt mirror, and on the wall opposite, a large oil painting showing buttocky nude females—nymphs, I assumed—bathing in a lily pond. There were damasked sofas, chairs with delicate curved legs, wall-to-wall floral carpeting, a pianoforte with gleaming white keys, busty statuettes of Venus, warbling caged canaries, and flowers everywhere. Yes, great vases erupting in roses and lilies and yellow and rust-colored chrysanthemums, effusing a subtle fragrance throughout. I had never seen flowers at Mrs. Hammond's. Her brownstone had always been just a mite stale. Here, everything was fresh.

And yet, something was off. I sat on a damasked ottoman, pondered. That painting of nymphs—a feast of warm, pink flesh—seemed better suited to a barroom in a fancy hotel. Mrs. Hammond's parlor, sumptuous as it was when uncovered, had conveyed a certain chaste elegance that was lacking here. Everything about this parlor—the paintings, the statuettes, the flowers—seemed a bit too assertive, too exuberant; a point was being made. Exactly: nothing had been left to chance; every last detail had been calculated. But to what end?

"Good morning, Mr. Fox," a vibrant voice pealed from the doorway, as a woman of uncertain age, handsomely preserved, walked in. Her full figure was richly encased in brocade, her dark hair was drawn back in a Niagara of curls, and her jeweled hand clasped an eagle-feather fan. Like her parlor, she struck me as a marvel of artifice.

I rose quickly. "Good morning, Mrs. Clayborn. I hope I haven't come too early."

"That's quite all right. Early for us but not for you, no doubt. The girls aren't even up yet."

No mention of a husband; a widow with daughters, I assumed.

She sat on the ottoman, waved me to an armchair facing it. "Please tell me of your experience."

I recounted my education and my years at Downing's and at Mrs. Hammond's, with special emphasis on my mastery of the brownstone's hot-air furnace, coal grates, and kerosene lamps, and my familiarity with the ritual of genteel dining. As I talked, she beat the air gently with the eagle-feather fan gripped in her ringed, tight fist.

"Excellent!" she announced. "Such tasks would be left to the waiter, but as butler you would supervise. You have no objection to somewhat late hours, I assume?"

"None at all."

"What references can you offer?"

"Mrs. Hammond is deceased, but she left a recommendation with her lawyer, Mr. Cyrus Webb of Webb & Willard. He can also recommend me, since he got to know me during the settlement of the estate."

"Were there bequests to servants?"

"Yes, to all of us."

"That speaks well of you. By all means have Mr. Webb write me."

"I shall."

"Normally, for the position of butler I would prefer someone older, but your experience is impressive, and your appearance and deportment satisfactory. You would be paid twelve dollars a week and have Monday, our slow day, off. The work requires a great deal of discretion. You must observe everything and report to me any irregularities. This establishment is the finest of its kind in the city. I have worked hard to make it so. The gentlemen callers must be screened at the door, and the girls overseen at all times. That will be your prime task."

At last it sank in, what Lester hadn't bothered to tell me: I was in a whorehouse—the fanciest one in the city! Mrs. Clayborn was the notorious Madam Ida, the abomination of pulpits and the toast of gaming houses, a newcomer who in no time at all had vaulted to the peak of ill fame! What had I got myself into?

"Well then," she said, rising, "I shall await Mr. Webb's letter. Give your address to Thelma, who will show you out. You'll hear from me. Good morning. I think we shall get on."

I rose and bowed, she left. Thelma reappeared with my hat and walking stick, took my address, then led me back down to the basement door, where she smiled and saw me out. Her smile—gracious but noncommittal—stayed with me as I trudged off down the street in a daze.

❦

I wrote Mr. Webb, requesting the references, then all week debated in my mind. Should I or shouldn't I? Would Mr. Webb realize to whom he was sending them? Would he care? And what kind of a reference would I have, if I ever left this woman's service? And was this the job I wanted—a butler in a whorehouse? And was this the brownstone I had longed for, this palace furnished more for a show of opulence than taste?

Yet the whole idea enticed me. After the funereal silence and gloom of Mrs. Hammond's, wouldn't this be a feast of life? I had learned long since that the world was more complicated than the Paradigms of Vice and Virtue suggested. Those who started out on one path might well end up on the other, or on yet another path undreamed of. And having seen the lords of creation being shorn and shaved at my father's barbershop, and having watched them gulping oysters at Downing's, how could I not pursue them into their clandestine den of pleasure? By the time I was done, few of their secrets would escape me.

And Madam Ida . . . What kind of a woman would run the city's most elegant brothel? Who was she, and how did she come to this? What kind of girls did she offer?

And Thelma—gracious yet distant, charming but reserved—wasn't she the greatest enticement of all? She had a mystery about her that I longed to discover, like a whorled shell that, if held to the ear, yields the sound of the sea. I had a sudden craving for the sea.

The pay was good, the job a challenge; I jumped at it.

# 12

ONE WEEK LATER I MOVED IN. I HAD EXPECTED A small, ill-heated servant's room with a dormer window under the mansard roof, but instead I was given the fairly large back bedroom on the fourth floor, with a view of a garden below. To my amazement, the hot-air furnace heated the whole building, and my adjoining bathroom had hot and cold running water. Never before had I lived like this. Clearly, to be a butler in such a house was a privilege.

Late that first morning, having arranged my things in my room, I went down to report to Madam Ida in the back room of the parlor floor, a library with green damask curtains, a massive oak mantelpiece, and sturdy glass-fronted walnut bookcases, their shelves lined solidly with books that struck me as out of place in a brothel. She sat at a writing desk with gilt decoration and curved legs, making lists and checking accounts. She simply repeated her general instructions to me, telling me to consult Thelma on matters of detail, which I was only too happy to do.

Thelma, the upstairs maid, was also Madam Ida's personal maid, though she worked downstairs as well, when the parlor maid was off. Obviously, she had Madam Ida's complete confidence. I thought she might feel threatened by my arrival, but no, she was always gracious and helpful. She was in charge of the upstairs floors, whereas I was to oversee the parlor floor, the kitchen and dining room in the basement, and the furnace in the cellar; of course we would work together.

During that first quiet morning, when the girls were still in their rooms, Thelma introduced me to the other servants, all black: the cook, waiter, parlor maid, coachman, and groom. The groom, Dennis, accompanied Madam Ida when she sortied in her carriage, but also doubled as houseman, helping Philip, the waiter, with heavy work like shifting furniture and filling up the coal bin—grimy work that I was glad to be relieved of. Dennis also looked after the garden in back.

"They're good workers," Thelma told me, "but you need to keep an eye on them. Don't ever let them squabble among themselves. Madam Ida can't stand that."

Thelma also gave me a quick sketch of Madam Ida's arrangements. The seven girls in residence had been carefully selected from a waiting list. They were young but not too young, and had experience; Ida didn't want rank beginners. They paid her room and board—no one knew how much, since she swore each one to secrecy, but certainly a hefty sum. This gave them the right to receive callers in the most prestigious bagnio in the city. They could receive in the parlor in the afternoon by appointment, otherwise they assembled in the parlor every evening at eight, after which gentlemen callers came with an appointment or, more often, without. The girls were responsible for their wardrobe, though when a new arrival of great promise came with little money, Ida might advance a sum for her wardrobe, expecting to be paid back with interest—an arrangement that usually worked out well for both. The girls left their earnings with Ida, who first deducted their room and board, then deposited their savings in a bank. Ida's ledger and spare cash were locked in the top drawer of her desk. She kept careful accounts, Thelma assured me; the girls were never cheated.

Needless to say, I itched to behold the seven beauties in residence, but during that first day I barely glimpsed their blurred forms scurrying past me in a hallway, and when I had lunch and supper in the kitchen with the help, I only heard a murmur of conversation from the adjoining dining room, where they were dining with Madam Ida. At lunch Ida had me stick my nose in so she could introduce me, but this momentary glimpse of a mix of young faces hardly prepared me for their entry into the parlor that evening.

At eight sharp the polished silver knocker on the door began rapping. Wearing black velvet with a white cravat, I assumed my duties as screener, squinting through an iron peephole to see if the callers, the first of the evening, were decently dressed and sober, in accordance with Madam Ida's insistence on strict decorum; they were. Admitting the gentlemen, I had them give their outer apparel to Dennis, who hung it on pegs in the hallway. Then I ushered them into the front parlor with its lyric birdcages, nymphs in oil, and flower-gushing urns, where the hostess awaited them in sumptuous brocade, icicled with diamonds and wielding her eagle-feather fan.

The callers were mostly older. Some of them I had whisked off at my father's barbershop, or opened oysters for at Downing's, but if they recognized me, they gave no sign. Orders for drinks were placed with Philip the waiter, then Madam Ida, tugging on a velvet bell cord, announced to her mustachioed guests, some of whom were new to the establishment, "Gentlemen, I offer you a pleiade of beauties, graduates of the most select female academies, lured, alas, by scoundrels to the city, undone, abandoned. I help them as I can."

And in the fair ones came. Standing at a distance so as to be on call, I saw the parade of full, ruffled skirts and low-necked bodices, their fine-boned oval faces as exquisite and dry as china. Each tried subtly to stand out: one in ruffled blue taffeta with soulful eyes; another in cold green silk, with spit curls plastered on her forehead; another in a mauve dress flounced with laces, looking like a frosted amethyst; another with a red rose in her bosom; another, her hair crimped to death, with a teasing hint of a smile; still another all in virginal white, her dress buttoned up to her chin, gloved, with a gardenia in her hair. When they had all been seated, the seventh, a chesty blonde, staged her carefully timed late entrance, appearing in gold-embroidered black satin, with twinkly gems and little jeweled birds in her hair, eliciting from the gentlemen an audible and admiring "Ah!" Clearly, she was the bright star of the pleiade that night.

Small talk followed.

"Have the gentlemen attended the theater? The new comedy by Mr. Malone is said to be delightful."

"Have the gentlemen read the latest novel by Mr. Wilkie Collins? *The Lady in White* is quite engrossing."

"Have the gentlemen been to the Central Park? The autumn colors are now just at their peak."

The gentlemen smiled, nodded, murmured, tapped their jeweled fingers, stroked their waxed imperials. The talk slowed, faltered to a stop, was revived through the efforts of the ladies. Madam Ida occasionally commented, wielding her eagle-feather fan. Summoned to the door to admit more guests, I returned to find the girl in virginal white at the pianoforte, while the one in blue taffeta sang a sentimental song of the day. Then the late arrival in gold-embroidered black satin recited "Tears, Idle Tears" by Mr. Tennyson. When she concluded with the lines "Deep as first love, and with all regret; / O Death in Life, the days that are no more," not an eye in the room was dry. This welling up of feeling in a parlor where everything was cunningly contrived, amazed me. It could have been the most respectable middle-class residence, with the widowed mother chaperoning her daughters and their gentlemen callers.

After further recitations and small talk, several gentlemen asked to be formally introduced to one or another young lady; their hostess obliged. Gradually the group broke up into separate tête-à-têtes, all still quite proper, no gentleman presuming to even furtively touch his companion. And yet, ushering more arrivals into the parlor, I felt uneasy, even repelled, at the sight of one of these exquisitely fragile young things—not one was over twenty-two—joined in conversation with some aging swain who, for all his shimmering watch chain and lace-trimmed linen shirt, had fat, hairy hands, a fleshy neck, skin yellow as old letters, or a veiny nose.

One by one, the young ladies began ushering their admirers upstairs to their rooms. Some gentlemen lingered, chatting with Madam Ida; more than once I heard her assure them, "This is the house of youth." Later, passing the doorway to the library, where a fire was blazing on the hearth, I observed several callers settled in armchairs, each engrossed in a book. When the scene was repeated on subsequent evenings, I realized with amazement that some of Madam Ida's high-paying guests simply craved a quiet, cozy atmosphere where they could get away from their families and relax.

After one in the morning I was not to answer the door. By two most of the guests, having settled with the hostess, had left, and I was allowed to retire, first locking up the liquor cabinet in the middle room. A few callers, having paid extra for the privilege, were allowed to spend the night. They would leave early in the morning, discreetly, without breakfast. Back in my fourth-floor room, I felt excited, disturbed, exhausted. What sweaty cleavings were occurring in those silent chambers behind thick, paneled doors, I preferred not to ponder. Falling into bed, I slept eight hours straight.

❧

"Junius, you got a job, and a good one! I'm just so glad! Dilly and I, we prayed to the Lord in heaven."

Needless to say, I didn't explain to Aunt Bessie just what their prayers had wrought.

"Where is Aunt Dilly, by the way?"

"She got a bee in her bonnet about quiltin'—a quiltin' bee. She and some ladies from the church get together to quilt. Mostly, I think they likes to gossip."

Just then Aunt Dilly arrived with a big bag full of quilting.

"Junius, I just can't wait to show you some quilts!"

"Dilly," said Bessie, "don't be botherin' the boy about that. Why should he be interested?"

"But I *am*," I insisted. "Show me, Aunt Dilly."

Out of the bag came scraps of bright-colored cloth that spilled out on the floor, then a half-finished quilt with squares and circles and triangles that were blue, red, pink, yellow, green: a blast of vibrant colors.

"Dilly," said Bessie, "look at the mess you're makin'." She stooped to gather up the scraps.

Dilly had spread the unfinished quilt on a table, exhibiting it proudly. "This says how I feel, when I'm singin' and prayin' at the church."

"Aunt Dilly, it's beautiful!"

"Come along to the bedroom, Junius. I show you one that's finished."

In her bedroom she spread another quilt out on the bed. Its frames were filled with chunky little figures suggesting people and animals and plants. "This a Bible quilt, Junius. See there, that's the Creation. There's Noah and the Ark and the animals. And here, that's Adam and Eve."

In the frame she pointed to, a stocky Adam was receiving an apple from a stocky Eve beside a tall, dark tree and a serpent with bright green eyes.

"This is wonderful, Aunt Dilly—I had no idea." The more I looked at it, the more I discovered. "It's beautiful, absolutely beautiful!"

Dilly teared. "Junius, I been waitin' all my life to hear someone say that somethin' I done was beautiful!" Now the tears were gushing.

Perception dawned in me: Dilly had always lived in her sister's shadow and had been taken for granted by everyone. Now she stood before me as an artist.

"Aunt Dilly, how did you ever learn to do this?"

"From your grandmomma, who died before you was born. After she passed, somehow I got away from it. But now the church ladies got me back into it, and we're just quiltin' up a storm!"

When we went back downstairs, Bessie said nothing but gave us a glowering look. When I left, Dilly saw me to the door.

"Your momma," she whispered, "she was called to the healin'. Me, I been called to the quiltin'. Poor Bessie, she screech her lungs out in the choir, but she ain't been called to nothin'."

She kissed me, waved good-bye, and winked.

When I returned two weeks later, Dilly announced that she had started a Freedom quilt, telling how black people had got free. Then, as I was leaving, she handed me a bag.

"Here, Junius, I gift you with this. It's the Bible quilt I showed you."

"Aunt Dilly, I couldn't take that. Months of work went into it. I'll bet someone would give good money for it."

"Don't want money, Junius. I want someone I love to have it. It'll keep you warm and safe. Lots of zigzags in it. Devils only go in straight lines; zigzags keep them out."

In my room that night I spread out Dilly's quilt on my bed. It was all wrong for a brownstone—too bold, too simple, too bright. But it pulsed with life; I loved it.

# 13

Every house has its mystery. At Mrs. Hammond's the shrouded parlor had obsessed me, until at last I was able to view it. In the mansion on East Thirty-eighth Street, it was Madam Ida. Who was she, where was she from? What had made her want to become the madam of the fanciest bordello in the city?

As the upstairs maid, Thelma spent a lot of time in a linen closet on the second floor, folding laundry from a basket and storing it neatly on the shelves. It was one of the few places where we could talk without interruption. I dropped by fairly often, as much to breathe her soothing fragrance as to garner information.

"Thelma, does Madam Ida ever talk about her past?"

"Never."

"Any idea where she's from?"

"I haven't a clue. All I know is that she's been in the city about two years."

"Is she a widow?"

"No idea. Say, aren't you getting nosy? What's up?"

"She's an interesting person. I'd like to know more about her."

"In this business, the less you know about anyone's past, the better."

"Well, if she ever drops a hint, let me know."

"There won't be many. But I'll tell you one thing: she hates men."

"How can she? She's ever the genial hostess, and she panders all the time to their taste."

"She hates them."

"She doesn't hate me, I'd sense it."

"You don't count. You're black."

"How do you know she hates them?"

But Thelma clammed up.

❧

"Junius, I have a very great favor to ask of you." Madam Ida was sitting at her desk in the library, where she had summoned me. "This may be the last of the good autumn weather, and I simply must take a drive in the Park. Dennis is indisposed. Would you terribly mind attending me as groom? That is not the function of a butler, but I'm desperate."

Something was up; I wanted to be in on it. "I'd be glad to, Miz Ida. I could use a turn in the Park."

"I will be eternally grateful. Thelma will bring you Dennis's livery. You're about the same size; it should fit."

An hour later I was waiting by the carriage in front, top-hatted, wearing a dark frock coat and tan leggings tucked into polished black boots. When Madam Ida appeared in a satin-striped dress, staunchly whaleboned, under a huge hat wreathed with roses, in one hand she held a blue parasol trimmed with black lace, and in the other a lorgnette with a jeweled handle. She nodded to me; I handed her into the carriage, then sprang up to the rumble seat in back, sat down facing forward, and folded my arms and stared straight ahead in the approved manner for grooms. When John the coachman gave a snap of his whip, and the horses started off, I had the feeling that all of us were actors playing roles in a farce.

Soon we were clippetyclopping up the Fifth Avenue. Just beyond the unfinished walls of St. Patrick's Cathedral, we passed a handsome brownstone at Fifty-second Street with spacious grounds around it; Madam Ida scrutinized it with her jeweled lorgnette. Soon afterward we were on the Drive in the Park, where riders of both sexes and carriages of every description were parading past ponds with gliding swans, a bubbly fountain, and groves whose thinning foliage was splotched with red and orange. All the fancy white folks were there, to see and be seen. Eyeing it all from my perch, I was hugely entertained.

At one point Madame Ida signaled John to stop. Springing down from my seat, I handed her out of the carriage.

"Thank you," she said. "I will stroll for a little. Tell John to follow."

As she promenaded on a walk near the Drive, I reassumed my perch, and the carriage followed her slowly at a distance. Other promenaders had also stepped down from their carriages. It was a rich mix of parasols and top hats nodding graciously to one another and sometimes stopping to chat. No one greeted Ida.

Suddenly the crowd parted as a woman in a brocaded dress with a green parasol advanced. As she and Ida met, watched by all, they paused, nodded civilly, then continued on their separate ways. Not a word had been spoken, but there was tension in the air.

When Ida returned to her carriage, I helped her in and resumed my seat, and we rejoined the parade on the Drive. Minutes later we met the lady with the green parasol riding in the opposite direction, attracting much attention with her finery and her silver-harnessed team, one black, one white, driven by a mulatto coachman magnificent in red and gold livery. Again their eyes met and they exchanged a cool, brief, noncommittal nod. On the other woman's face, which this time I could see quite clearly, I detected the faintest hint of a smile. The meaning of this pantomime escaped me.

❧

"Give me a report," said Thelma, motioning me into the linen closet the following morning.

I told her of the woman with the green parasol, whom Ida had nodded to twice.

"Did she have a mulatto coachman in red and gold livery?"

"Yes."

"That's Madame Restell, the Lady of Solutions."

The name didn't register.

"The town's most notorious abortionist."

Now it clicked. Everyone knew of Madame Restell, who had plied her trade for decades, denounced by moralists but sought out by married women weary of childbearing, and unmarried women dreading disgrace. Her latest offense was to have built a brownstone palace on the Avenue, right smack in the most exclusive residential district in the city.

"So, it was Restell's brownstone that she was eyeing with her lorgnette at Fifty-second Street."

"Of course, she's jealous. Ida has this fancy brownstone, but Restell has a whole freestanding house with grounds all around it. And at least four carriages; Ida has just one. They've been at it now for a year."

"At what?"

"Facing each other down in public, trying to make a finer show. That's why she needed you yesterday. Restell has a coachman, but Ida has a groom as well."

"But they're not really competitors. Professionally, Restell gets the ladies of the carriage trade, and Ida gets the men."

"Restell wants it all. When she and her husband built their brownstone, they had a housewarming, invited lots of bigwigs and their wives. Ida hoped for an invitation, didn't get one. If you're out to snag respectables, you can't toss in the madam of a whorehouse, even if it's the fanciest one in town. So now Restell's practicing her trade on the Avenue and flaunting herself in her carriage."

"You'd think they'd be natural allies."

"Junius, you don't know women. There's room for only one illicit lady at the top. Restell has it, Ida wants it, and the whole town's watching."

"Thelma, where did you ever learn a word like 'illicit'?"

She smiled. "I'm a schoolteacher's brat."

Which was the first thing she'd ever said about herself. She was just as much a mystery as Ida.

Since Madam Ida proclaimed her brownstone a "house of youth," everything had to be fresh. First thing in the morning, the parlor maid Julie removed any traces of the previous evening's revels, smoothed the upholstery, plumped and straightened pillows, wiped surfaces, swept, and dusted. The canaries were fed, their cages cleaned. All flowers were removed and discarded, and their receptacles scrubbed, since Ida had a horror of smelly vases; by ten, fresh flowers had been delivered by the florist. Meanwhile Philip the waiter had tended the furnace in the cellar, delivered coal to the kitchen stove, removed the ashes in the library fireplace, and toted trash out to the curb. Instructed by Ida, I then inspected the entire parlor floor, looking for any stained fabric or raveled fringe, any faint trace of cigar ash; rarely was anything amiss. Philip was a shy young man, very diligent, who needed only a little attention. Julie, a friend of Thelma's, was a sweet young thing who needed lots. The moment I complimented her on her work, she brightened:

"Oh thank you, Junius. I just drink up kindness."

As with the furnishings, so with the girls; they had to be presentable by lunchtime, attractive by afternoon, and radiant by evening. Since I used the servants' back stairs and they used the front, I rarely saw them by day. Their conversation at lunch, which I could hear from the kitchen, was obsessed with skirt ruffles and pagoda sleeves and flounces, citing the latest issue of *Godey's Lady's Book* or the *Journal des Demoiselles.* Hoopskirts, I learned, were totally passé, and there was a passionate debate about the braided hems and filigree buttons said to be favored by the Empress of the French.

What finicky preparations they underwent behind the paneled doors of their chambers I could only imagine.

Thelma, who had daily access to their rooms, told me of whalebone and wire-hoop skirt supporters, of bust forms of cotton padding and inflated rubber, of spiral-spring bosom pads, and pompadours and waterfalls and braids filled out with imported horse hair from South America—more than any male ought to know. She told me too of applications to the skin of white rice powder, of lemon juice, and of rosemary mixed with white wine. One young beauty rubbed her face with minced raw meat to acquire an alabaster complexion. To achieve the same, another sneaked down to the garden to roll naked in the morning dew, a performance I never managed to catch. Whatever the preparations, their parlor entrance always astonished.

I studied them. Their appearance was dazzling, their manners flawless, their conversation remarkably genteel. Whatever entertainments the city offered, they could speak of them knowingly. They fluttered their fans deftly, received compliments graciously, never teased or flirted. Whether their company was sought by a hale young stud or a whiskered gentleman of years—and it was usually the latter—they never lost their poise. They had the sheen of youth, but never a flash of feeling, a burst of spontaneity; they smiled but never laughed. All was rehearsed, all was calculated. Only when they sang or recited did they betray a hint of feeling, a plaintive longing for childhood's sunny hour that was quickly masked. I called them the "china dolls."

It took me a while to sort the seven out: Gladys of the soulful eyes, Doris of the spit curls, Elaine with the little jeweled birds in her hair, and so on. When our paths crossed, they nodded politely and addressed me by name, but there was no warmth. Far from being attracted to them, I found them cold and distant. Emily, the one all in white, reminded me of the lacy white core of an ice cube.

I shared my reaction with Thelma. "It's almost as if they were frightened of me."

"They are."

"But why?"

She smiled, said nothing.

It became clear when Madam Ida addressed Thelma and me in the library: "I am quite pleased with your service, but I wish to reiterate certain things. A girl who was once with us and then removed to another establishment has just been expelled from there for using drugs, the very reason why she had to leave here. We must be vigilant. Any use of drugs, or excessive use of alcohol, cannot be tolerated. For that matter, any impertinence is not permitted, or any prolonged blue sulks, or any hint of the jaded. Our girls must be fresh, bright, and cheerful. Please report any behavior that is detrimental. I count on you. You are my eyes and ears."

No wonder the girls were scared of me; they saw me as a spy!

I had settled into the brownstone, knew its routines. Leaving Marie the cook to rule in the kitchen, where she produced culinary marvels far surpassing the fare at my previous brownstone, I felt myself in full possession of the parlor floor. In quiet moments I breathed the scent of ever fresh flowers, touched the oak mantel of the library and the marble fireplaces of the parlor, caressed damask and velvet and silk.

Serenaded by canaries, I studied those brazen nude bathers on the wall, touched the cold marble flesh of a Venus in the half-light filtered through ferns and vines hanging in a window. Every stand, every whatnot had yielded to my probing eye its fragile offering of stuffed birds under glass, dried butterflies, wax flowers, or a sea shell inscribed with the words "Gather ye rosebuds while ye may." But the bedrooms escaped me.

Ah, the bedrooms . . . As butler I had the run of the house, but the upstairs floors were Thelma's domain, and I was rarely needed there. The second, third, and fourth floors each had three large bedrooms and two small ones; the large ones were allotted to Ida, the girls, and me, and the small ones to the rest of the help. The girls' rooms and Ida's could be latched from within; the help's could not be. It was a rule of the house that no one should enter someone else's room in their absence, except for Thelma and me in the course of our duties; to date I had never done so. But I was curious, having once again detected a whiff of mystery from that domain of womankind that I seemed always to be on the fringe of.

"Thelma, what are the girls' bedrooms like?"

"During the day, some messy, some neat as a pin. Shimmering silks, bonnets on pegs, mirrors, scraps of embroidery, ribbons and dollies, fans, flounces, braid. One of them has a mirror on the ceiling, please don't ask me why. But none of them is any match for Ida's."

"Really? Show me."

"I should have known you'd ask."

"What's the harm?"

"She doesn't want people poking about."

"I won't touch a thing, just look. C'mon, be a sport."

"And what if she comes in?"

"I'm there to check the heating, or shift a wardrobe so you can clean behind it."

She shook her head.

"Thelma, we live in a world of white folks; I want to know what makes them tick. I want to know how they live, what fabrics and baubles they surround themselves with, all the things they smell and feel. I want to know everything I can about their brownstones."

She looked right at me, her gray-green eyes flecked with gold. "You're a strange man. I've never known anyone like you."

"So, when can I have a look?"

"Two o'clock. She'll be going to the bank then, and does she have a lot to deposit!"

Every other day Madam Ida went by carriage to the Bank of New York on Wall Street, taking her own and the girls' earnings in a pouch of Russian leather. This parade, noticed by everyone, told the city just how well she was doing. Sometimes she took one of the girls with her and had her wait in the carriage while she did her business inside: a stunning advertisement for the delights that her establishment offered.

At two that afternoon we met outside the door; Thelma led me in. My eye went straight to the bed, a towering four-poster with carved mahogany posts and rose-colored silk damask hangings with a cream silk lining, and a counterpane of blue brocade. I stared, then touched, caressed the fabrics and wood, till Thelma pulled me back.

"Quite something, isn't it?" she said.

"It's rich and royal and magnificent. I've never seen anything like it." I stroked the counterpane again and inhaled a subtle fragrance of lavender and mint, till Thelma removed my hand.

"At Restell's housewarming," said Thelma, "the whole house was open for inspection, and journalists reported a handsome bedstead of ebony and gold. But that one can't hold a candle to this."

"What it must be—the feeling of grandeur and bliss—to sleep every night in a bed like that! It would tell you your life is worth living."

"You might as well see the bathroom, too."

Following her into it, I discovered gleaming silver-plated faucets and polished porcelain, the air perfumed by powders and soaps. The tub was a monument in marble, and the commode a sculptured porcelain dolphin rising from the sea. I looked, I sniffed, I touched. What emperor enjoyed such luxury?

"All right, you've had your glimpse of wonderland. Now clear out before you cost us both our jobs!"

Once again I ran my hand over the cold, smooth marble of the tub. Then, with great reluctance, I let her shoo me out. Now I was more curious than ever about the woman whose luxurious nest I had just inspected.

From then on, grandiose nocturnal fantasies possessed me. The bed as bed of state where Ida, then Thelma, regally reclined. The bed as litter bearing Thelma/Queen of Sheba

(I'd been reading the Bible) into the lordly presence of Solomon, whom she showered with gifts of spices and gold. The bed as silver-oared barge gliding over the waters of the Nile, taking Thelma/Cleopatra (I'd been reading Shakespeare) toward a dazzled, smitten Antony. Or as a chariot, or a flying carpet, or a full-rigged ship with billowing sails of blue brocade. But always there was Thelma, bejeweled and perfumed, smiling radiantly, who gazed at me, winked, then mischievously crooked her finger, till Junius/Solomon/Antony advanced rapturously, mounting a magnificent erection. These imaginings enriched me with a bubbling of joy, a kindling of hope, and a blast of seed.

Alas, by day my own room seemed no fit residence for Junius/Solomon/Antony, being bleak and bare, redeemed only by the color from Aunt Dilly's quilt. Learning from Thelma of a cellar storeroom next to the furnace to which Ida relegated discarded items that were the casualties of earlier refurbishings, I got her to take me there; lamp in hand, I explored its dusty treasures. Since Thelma admitted to having spirited away a few small objects to brighten her own room, I decided to sneak some items up the back stairs to mine.

"You're crazy!" said Thelma, perversely unaware of her role as Sheba/Cleopatra.

"You did it yourself."

"Not like this. You're taking too much."

"Just a few things. It's not stealing. None of the stuff will ever leave the brownstone. It's just a redistribution of spoils."

"You're absolutely crazy!"

Maybe I was, just a little: the more I took, the more I wanted. By the time I finished, my once barren room boasted a small floral rug; blue silk window curtains; two ornate flower vases; a hassock that whoofed when you sat on it (a "pouf," said Thelma); an easy chair and a lamp to read by; a whatnot that I vowed to clutter up; bronze bookends with the inscription "My Library Was Dukedom Large Enough—Shakespeare," which I hoped to put to good use; a crystal candelabrum with tinkling prisms; and cushions galore. For a final touch, when the parlor urns were renewed each morning, I claimed some of the discarded flowers, which showed hardly a trace of age, to fill my empty vases and freshen the top-floor air. In such rich surroundings I could live fully, yearn grandly. At last I had truly moved in; I had my silken nest.

# 14

BECAUSE PHILIP THE WAITER MIGHT ON OCCASION need help in serving the guests, Madam Ida initiated me into the mysteries of mixed drinks, which I knew little about, since Mrs. Hammond's intake had been confined to sherry, and my own to cheap beers and ales. Ida herself showed me how to concoct a whiskey cobbler, a hot toddy, a gin sling, and how to serve Madeira, stout, and cognac. Banned from the premises were any drinks that she deemed "common": applejack, hard cider, cheap whiskey, most beers and ales, typical offerings of the city's saloons. God help the guest who requested such refreshment in her parlor. Mastering these intricacies gave me a heightened sense of power, a further insight into the ways of the white elite.

I no longer looked forward to my visits to Minetta Lane, given Bessie's sour view of Dilly's quilting. But when I saw them close to Christmas, all was sweetness and light.

"Junius," Bessie announced, "you are lookin' at the number-one best children's storyteller of the Greater New Tabernacle Baptist Church."

"That's true," said Dilly. "She's just a wonder with children."

"How did it happen, Aunt Bessie?"

"There's this teacher lady at church always tellin' how the little children don't pay her no mind, they all just wild and destructious. So, I said, 'Now Minnie, I have a touch with children; let me try my hand.' So, I went to the school and sure enough, come nap time, the children were just jumpin' around and sassed her somethin' wild. So, I said, 'Now children, sit on your mats and listen, 'cause Aunt Bessie's gonna tell you a story.' That got their attention, 'cause children like stories. So, I told them about Noah and the Ark, and Daniel in the lions' den, and all those things in Dilly's Bible quilt. And the children just lambed out and behaved so pretty, and finally, one by one, they all just fell asleep. And I did, too. When nap time was over and Minnie woke us all up, I just laughed and laughed, 'cause I been snoozin', too. But Minnie asked me to come every week and tell them a story, and that's what I'm gonna do, that bein' the onliest way to calm down fractious children."

"What kind of stories will you tell, Aunt Bessie?"

"More Bible stories. And stories about our family, how your poppa snip-snipped the white folks for years, and how your momma did the healin'. And stories from Dilly's Freedom quilt, that she's workin' at so neat and hard. Oh, I've got lots of stories!"

Later I saw Dilly's Freedom quilt, with frames showing hulls of crowded slave ships, and black people working in the fields under a whip, and stations on the Underground Railroad, and everyone making jubilee when President Lincoln issued his proclamation. This quiet old woman, who had always seemed so wrapped up in her church work and aware of little else, had the whole history of her race locked up there inside her, felt it to her bones, and now expressed it in bursts of color; I was humbled.

This time it was Bessie who saw me to the door. "Junius," she said, "I been a hard woman all my life. It's time I softened up."

To my surprise, business on Christmas Eve at Madam Ida's was brisk; Ida donated all the proceeds to charity. Otherwise, the holiday was not particularly observed there, though behind more than one of the china dolls' doors I detected what sounded like sobs—a tribute to the memories of childhood. But New Year's was another matter.

"The receiving of gentlemen callers on New Year's Day is a time-honored tradition in the city," Ida informed her assembled staff. "I and the young ladies have sent out numerous invitations. We anticipate some sixty callers, all of them distinguished gentlemen prominent in the city's affairs. To receive them properly will require the utmost effort by all of us. Rare delicacies, fine wines, and conversation will be the only entertainment offered."

Which meant that, on this one occasion, the girls would be receiving only in the parlor; there would be no forays upstairs.

"She's competing with Restell," Thelma confided to me later. "Restell's New Year's Day receptions are notorious. She's said to get at least fifty callers; Ida hopes for more."

The thought of the town's big bugs being fought over socially by the town's most successful abortionist and its most affluent and exclusive brothel keeper perked me up no little.

By noon of New Year's Day, while Ida and the girls were still primping upstairs, the staff, after laborious preparations, were putting the last touches to the display in the parlor. Gas chandeliers glowed, oak logs crackled in the fireplaces, bronze and marble and woodwork shone, and silver candlesticks gleamed. Masses of red and yellow roses on stands exhaled their freshness everywhere. On the sideboard in the middle room towered two huge burnished silver urns, one for coffee and one for tea, with china cups, polished silverware, and gleaming gold-rimmed crystal goblets. There were decanters of port and Madeira; fruit bowls heaped high with lady apples and oranges and Malaga grapes; cut-glass dishes with sweetmeats; and a dazzling array of nuts, dates, figs, and raisins, and mince pie, plum cake, ginger pudding, and blackberry tarts.

Outside it was a bright, cold day with patches of dirty snow on the ground and a brisk wind; just the weather to whet a caller's appetite and make him yearn for warmth. With callers expected from one o'clock on, the china dolls appeared at about a quarter of, all fixed up in taffeta and satin and silk adorned with tucks and flounces. Cameos or brooches shone above their low-cut bodices; diamonds twinkled in their hair; their ringed fingers fluttered ivory or tortoiseshell fans.

Scarcely had I absorbed this sight, when Madam Ida herself appeared, fresh from the hands of her hairdresser, who for an exorbitant fee had just attended her upstairs. She entered smiling radiantly, a monument in blue brocade, her massed hair (real and false) swept back and cascading in curls, while the strokes of her eagle-feather fan grazed a breastplate of jewels. All eyes turned; not one of the china dolls commanded such attention.

Minutes later the front door's silver knocker began sounding, and I found myself admitting a steady stream of visitors. First came the younger set intent on crowding in an incredible number of calls that day, followed later by the old hands, who were more selective and saved the most interesting hostesses and the most lavish spreads till last. After Dennis the houseman had taken the callers' wraps, I received their cards, ushered them into the front parlor, and announced them resonantly. Ida and the girls then welcomed them graciously and initiated small talk involving mutual compliments and appraisal of the weather. Meanwhile, having deposited the cards in a silver bowl on a stand in the hallway, I was supervising the help, until summoned again to the door by the knocker. At intervals Thelma and Julie brought refreshments from a dumbwaiter in the library, which was just above the kitchen, and Philip the waiter circulated among the guests with a tray of delicacies. As more callers arrived, the gentle murmur grew to a babble.

In the course of the afternoon I accumulated impressions of the richly bearded and fiercely mustached callers. (I myself, resisting the opinion of the times that facial hair was handsome and virile, had remained clean-shaven in the style of the fifties.) All those whom I recognized from earlier visits to the parlor—the great majority of callers—I had by now classified into three groups: bloods, senescents, and satyrs. The bloods were young men new to the scene and brimming with spunk, eager to confirm their manhood. Given Ida's prices, they were few in number; with them I had no quarrel. The senescents were rich, flagging seed-bearers obsessed with potency. These were Ida's preferred customers, fleshy-necked masters of the city's hurly-burly who, having everything, still needed her.

Finally, the satyrs: sex-obsessed hunters, old or young, leering out of snowy sideburns or staring with a hot, bold eye. They'd been at it since the cradle, pawing nursemaids and governesses in their younger years, incapable of glimpsing a woman without at once sexually appraising her, their whole self involved in the chase. Passing near a bunch of them chatting among themselves in a corner, I heard scraps of talk.

". . . She was walking with that steady, well-balanced step that indicates fleshy limbs and a fat backside. My dingus stood up at the sight of her . . ."

". . . She fetched me so God-awful fast, a proper poke it was!" "Why you old fuckster!" "Then later I learned that she had clapped me! . . ."

". . . This wine makes me randy. Look at that one over there—lithe as a willow branch. Oh God, I'm all spermed up, nigh bursting for a frig! . . ."

Their obsession struck me as mean, grubby, dull. For them I had the utmost contempt.

The regulars were soon clustered around the young ladies of their choice, mixing small talk with a gentle touch of flirting that the hostesses deftly ignored. But other callers were new to me. When I announced in quick succession, "Mr. William

Marcy Tweed . . . His Honor, Justice George G. Barnard . . . Mr. A. Oakey Hall," there was a stir throughout the parlor, and Madame Ida, breaking off a conversation with other guests, came toward them with an especially gracious smile.

Tweed, a massive man with a close-cropped reddish beard and a blue-white shirtfront diamond, spoke with a soft voice that charmed, and at times gave forth a deep and booming laugh. The judge, a dapper gentleman with wavy jet-black hair, eyed the girls like a connoisseur, while Hall, a short man with a black beard and mustache, an embroidered crimson vest, and pince-nez perched on his nose, pranced about nimbly, emitting witticisms and puns that brought forth smiles and titters from all. Later I learned from Thelma that Tweed was the rising power in Tammany; Barnard, his crony and a brandy-sipping scamp of a judge; and Hall, the current district attorney, a town wit and lecturer whom Tweed was grooming to be mayor. For Ida, quite a catch.

Another caller who arrived alone was fashionably but not ostentatiously dressed—the mark, I thought, of Old Money. When I announced "Mr. Charles Lohman" there was another slight stir in the room, and Ida greeted him with a cool civility that surprised me, given his smooth manner and smile. Soon he was chatting with Barnard and Hall and some of Ida's regulars, whom he seemed to know quite well. Thelma, passing with a tray, observed my interest and whispered, "Restell's husband." So, Ida had seen fit to invite her rival's spouse, and he had seen fit to come. Not Old Money, then, but a good imitation of it. I strained to catch snippets of his conversation. He discoursed genially on the niceties of billiards, the fine points of appraising horseflesh, and his impression of the port he was sipping: "A soft, round taste, quite mature." It was the talk of a gentleman.

"Do remember me to your wife," said Ida as he left.

"I surely will," he replied with a smile.

So, Ida's success would be reported in quarters where she most wanted it known.

Charles Lohman had struck me as something of a charmer, smooth, courteous, gallant—several notches above most of the regulars. Indeed, seen close up at Ida's, the lords of the city who had so dazzled me when I first glimpsed them in my father's shop and at Downing's, were now beginning to look petty and dull.

Since her rival's name had come up, Ida took full advantage. I heard her expounding to a circle of guests, many of whom had probably just come from Restell's residence on the Avenue.

"Her marble shines and her silks rustle, but her money is tainted, her touch is lethal; she lives in a palace of death. Here there is life and joy. The girls are as fresh as the flowers. Rest assured, gentlemen"—smiling over fresh-cut roses at a clutch of heavies well past their prime—"this is the House of Youth."

A great performance, a great lie; they hung on every word.

# 15

IT WAS A DREARY WINTER, MORE SLEET THAN SNOW, with an icy slush underfoot, and days of cold, gray rain; in my free time I holed up in my nest. Madam Ida, having noticed me returning with books from a colored lending library, invited me to sample the tomes on her library's glass-fronted shelves. Settling cozily in my easy chair beside the kerosene lamp, I devoured *Paradise Lost* and plunged deep into the plays of Shakespeare. Never had I been so snug and warm through the winter, so deliciously self-contained.

Though my contact with the china dolls was slight, they now seemed less distant, less suspicious. On one occasion Clara of the crimped hair addressed me in the hall:

"Junius, I have a teeny-tiny favor to ask."

"And what might that be, Miss Clara?"

"Come!"

She waved me into her room, where dresses, scarves, and bonnets lay everywhere; she was inspecting her wardrobe. Beckoning me over to a large mirror that tilted in its frame on her dresser, she asked, "Which is more becoming? This . . . ?" Deftly she piled her loose curls on top of her head, held them there a moment. "Or this . . . ?" Released, the curls tumbled down in a cascade of ringlets. "Which?"

"I really don't know, Miss Clara."

"Claire," she corrected. "I've decided to change my name. But you *must* know, this is very important. This . . . ?" She piled the curls up again. "Or this . . . ?" Again, she let them fall. "Which?"

"I know so little about these things, Miss Claire. Why don't you ask Thelma or the other girls?"

"Because I want a man's opinion. So, which, Junius, which?"

"Well, I guess I'm partial to ringlets."

"Thank you, Junius. Ringlets it shall be! And now just one more teeny-tiny favor. Which *chapeau* works with the ringlets? This . . . or this?"

She put on a bonnet trimmed with pink velvet and what looked like rosebuds and wheat, then removed it and put on another of black lace adorned with scarlet cherries and, nested in white blond leaves on top, a hummingbird. With all those dead things, I thought them both grotesque.

"I think the first, Miss Claire, though both are very becoming."

"Junius, you're a jewel. Now just one more teeny-tiny favor . . ." She began marshaling an array of shoes.

"I can't, Miss Claire. I've got to get back to my job."

With that, I decamped.

Later I recounted the incident to Thelma, who smiled knowingly.

"Watch out for those teeny-tiny favors; one thing leads to another. It's best to keep clear of the lot of them. Above all, don't ever let them even glimpse your room."

"Why not?"

"If they saw all that loot from the cellar, they might threaten to tell Ida. That would give them a hold on you; they could demand special favors."

This had never occurred to me. But I had learned my lesson. When Doris of the spit curls asked me to move her wardrobe, I moved it quickly and got out. When Gladys of the soulful eyes begged me to fetch a prescription from a druggist, offering to pay for the service, I smiled and declined. And when Emily, who dressed all in white, tried to tell me how spitefully Eva had treated her, I referred her to Madam Ida. After that, requests for teeny-tiny favors declined.

Returning from my day off one Monday, I learned from Thelma that chesty Elaine, who liked to sprinkle her hair with jeweled birds and gems, had been shown the door by Ida.

"Why?"

"Impertinence—I don't know the details. I'd seen it coming for a long time. That gold-embroidered black dress of hers was just a bit too showy."

"Aren't they supposed to get the men's attention?"

"Up to a point. But they must never upstage Ida. Elaine had been doing just that."

"What'll become of her?"

"She'll turn up at one of the pricier places, just a notch below Ida's. With luck, she'll be there a few more years. Then she'll be dismissed to one of the dingier houses and finally end up in some sailor-packed den near the docks. That's how it usually goes."

"Does it have to be like that?"

"Just about, if their families won't take them back. Some of them manage to get kept; one or two have even got married. But for most of them it's all downhill. The smart ones become madams."

This depressed me for days. Meanwhile Alice, a delicate brunette in fawn silk, moved in and was schooled by Ida in the parlor. "Be subtle," I heard her tell the girl. "Give interestingly, and with mystery. Satisfy, yet always suggest some hidden depth yet to be revealed." If Ida hated men, she also understood them.

All was fine until, a few nights later, screams from Alice's room resounded in the hall. Almost instantly Ida and I were knocking at the door, which someone unlatched; we entered. There was Alice, cowering on one side of the bed in her chemise, and there on the other side was her client, an alderman, standing in his drawers.

"He wants to hit me with *that*!" she stammered, pointing to a whip in the alderman's fist.

At Madam Ida's, such diversions were forbidden, unless the young lady consented.

"Nonsense!" asserted the client. "She misunderstood. I wanted *her* to whip *me*!"

Ida frowned mightily. "Alice, have you no experience? Such requests are routine. You won't be in any way harmed."

Dismissing me from the room, Ida talked to the girl at length, then rejoined me in the hall.

"Absolutely ridiculous! Satisfying male fantasies is what this is all about! Whips, chains, handcuffs—these are nothing but toys. Some men go that route, others crave a specific perfume or smell, a certain feel of fabric or color of underclothing; the possibilities are endless. The girl will have to learn." Then, relenting: "Well, she's young and new."

So ended the affair. I gleaned from it two insights: how varied the services the girls must provide, and how ludicrous an alderman looks in his drawers.

Late one evening, returning tired to my room, which could not be locked, I found a red rose on my pillow: a token of love, but from whom? Certainly not Thelma, not her style at all. Julie? Doubtful; there'd been no hint of anything between us. Marie the cook? She was engaged to the coachman, John. That left only the china dolls, not one of whom had shown an inclination. I shrugged, put the rose in a vase.

One week later I had a strange dream in the middle of the night. A woman had slipped into my room, tossed off her chemise, and lain down naked beside me, waking me gently as she kissed me, then pulled up my nightshirt and, as I stirred groggily, put her lips to my stiffening member, received it, and brought me to completion. I woke up dazed, alone. Only my disarranged nightshirt, my feeling of having spent, and a trace of perfume in the air told me I had not been dreaming.

In the morning I found another red rose on my pillow. Clear-headed, I took stock. Though I had been marvelously satisfied, I felt confused, exposed, almost violated. Who had been there? Obviously the giver of the rose. But who was she? Over the next week I studied the china dolls intensely, observing every expression, every remark, every gesture, without obtaining the slightest indication. Kathleen liked to wear roses in her bosom, but in all this time we had not exchanged five words; she was no more suspect than the others. I well knew what a bawdy tale Lester Hicks would have made of my adventure, but for me it was disturbing.

❧

Late that winter two incidents attended my duties as guardian of the threshold. The first involved young Richardson, the dissolute son of an eminently respectable insurance executive. The young man had already made a splash in the news by getting arrested for cavorting on the Avenue in the buff—drunk, of course—but he had always managed to pass muster at Ida's. One night, however, having entered reasonably sober, he availed himself of a hidden flask and was soon uproariously drunk, singing snatches of bawdy songs in the parlor.

"Junius," said Ida, "Mr. Richardson is under the influence. Please cope."

Even as she spoke, shouts and gasps were heard at the far end of the room, followed by a general exodus in our direction. Some of the men seemed to be smirking, but most of the faces registered shock. Proceeding to investigate, I found Richardson whistling blithely as he urinated into a blue delft Chinese bowl, a recent acquisition that Ida particularly prized.

"Junius," thundered Ida, "remove that man forthwith!"

Philip and I leaped to obey. As soon as he had retrieved his member, we seized him under the armpits, lifted him up, and carried him, his feet treading air, out of the parlor and the house, down the stoop, and to a point farther down the street, where we deposited him in a heap on the sidewalk. He was still babbling and singing as if nothing had happened. A patrolman approached and, when informed of the circumstances, took the offender into custody. Meanwhile Dennis had the joy of removing and emptying the bowl, while Ida, with a stern but gracious gaze, labored to restore decorum to the parlor.

The story swept the town. Three versions circulated: the culprit had committed his offense (1) (as witnessed by me) into a blue delft Chinese bowl, or (2) into a cannel coal fireplace, or (3) under a pianoforte, for which defilement Ida had banned him forever from the precincts of grace.

The second incident involved none other than Justice George G. Barnard of the Supreme Court of New York, whose dapper presence had honored us on New Year's Day. Accompanied by friends, he appeared at our door one evening sporting his usual white topper and a walking stick, but visibly drunk.

"Sir," I announced, "I'm afraid I must deny you the premises."

The judge was stunned. "Are you telling me I can't come in?"

"Yes sir. I respectfully suggest that you go home and sleep it off."

The judge flashed a look of rage. "Do you know who I am?"

"Yes sir."

"Nigger, you'll pay for this!"

He spun about and staggered down the stoop. His friends watched him wobble off, but being themselves presentable, elected to go in. Within minutes the affair had been whispered through the parlor. Philip and Dennis both gave me reports, with rumors of the judge's threatened vengeance. He was notoriously wrath-prone, spiteful, and arrogant, and as a chum of Boss Tweed's, had access to the highest levels of power. But having my orders, I stood my ground. Ida said not a word.

❧

No legal thunderbolt struck me the next day, or the day after that. Instead, a young man approached me on the street.

"Junius, the judge asked me to give you this." He held out an envelope.

"What is it?"

"A consideration."

"What kind of consideration?"

"One hundred dollars."

"What for?"

"To smooth things over. He wants to be readmitted to Ida's."

In point of fact, he hadn't been banned; but if he thought so, so much the better. "He owes me an apology."

"Do you know who you're dealing with?"

"I know exactly. Just tell him that from me."

I walked away.

Later I told Thelma; she gasped.

"Junius, that man has power. He'll want your head on a platter."

"Maybe, maybe not."

Ida summoned me, a severe look on her face. "Junius, I understand that there have been further developments with the judge."

"Yes ma'am."

"I understand that he has offered you one hundred dollars . . ."

"Yes ma'am."

". . . and you refused it."

"Yes ma'am."

She smiled. "Junius, you are incorruptible. I commend you. We will brook his wrath together."

The next day I got a note from the judge on official stationery: "Dear Junius, Let's clear this up. Come to my chambers at one on Monday—Barnard."

He was well informed; Monday was my day off.

"If you go," said Thelma, "take a toothbrush and a change of clothes. You may get clapped in jail."

I went, but without the toothbrush or clothes. At the courthouse on Centre Street a clerk showed me to the judge's chambers, a spacious room in black walnut with a chandelier, spittoons, and drapes, where His Honor received me behind a massive oak desk where he was whittling at a stick of pinewood, as he was known to do in court. A glass of brandy stood within easy reach. He rose to greet me and waved me to a seat.

"Junius, let's put all this behind us. Damn it, I want to return to Ida's. All my friends go there."

"Sir, I expect an apology."

"Oh damn it, we all make mistakes."

A silence; I eyed him coolly, waited. Black against white: who would yield?

He sighed. "Junius, I"—he took a deep breath—"apologize."

"Thank you, sir. Your apology is accepted."

"Now am I persona grata again?"

"That depends on Mrs. Clayborn."

"Will you put in a good word for me?"

"Certainly."

"That's all I ask. Thank you. Court's adjourned."

He smiled and waved me away. I had guessed right: the lure of Madame Ida's was stronger than spite or pride.

I saw Ida; the judge was welcomed again. He came often, noticeably sober, more to socialize than to taste the fruits of sin. Word raced through the city: Judge Barnard—the irascible, the arrogant—had apologized to the gatekeeping "nigger." From then on, in their dealings with me the gentlemen callers were courteous to a fault, even deferential. Power was mine.

# 16

SPRING CAME. ON MILD DAYS IN APRIL I OPENED MY bedroom windows and breathed a fragrance of lilac wafted up from the garden below. With Ida's permission, Thelma and I took short walks there, admiring the white and pink-purple clusters of blossoms and yellow blasts of daffodils, with tulips and iris pushing up, and rose bushes plumping tight buds.

"I love spring," said Thelma. "Can't you just feel roots thrusting down inside you, and grass blading up, and buds getting ready to burst?"

"Yes," I said with a smile. "I'm full of bursting buds."

"All right, make fun of me. But I love it. It's a time of new beginnings."

"*If* they're allowed to happen."

When we complimented Dennis, the houseman, who did the gardening, he was delighted. Ida strolled there rarely, the china dolls never.

I had my brownstone, but my possession was not complete—far from it: Thelma eluded me. I was as drawn to her as ever, but her relentless courtesy, with never a hint of encouragement, put me off. In her I sensed deep reserves of feeling that I longed to tap. She would give interestingly, and with mystery. Though I had visited ladies' boudoirs in their absence in the past, I had not explored Thelma's, having vowed to respect her privacy. But if I ever took her hand in the linen closet, she withdrew it with a whispered "no" and went on with her work. The more she held back, the more I wanted her; I was pretty worked up.

❧

Consolation was soon forthcoming. One night after I had retired and was almost asleep, my door opened softly and someone slipped in, removed her chemise, and again lay down naked beside me, kissing me gently, then satisfying me as she had done so marvelously the first time. I made no effort to reject her or to discover who she was; I simply yielded to the pleasure of it. Once again she left wordlessly, and once again I found a red rose on my pillow in the morning. It was weird and wonderful. Another scrutiny of the china dolls by day told me nothing. My Lady of the Rose, my Visitant, my Doodlebug. If this was the path to hell, it had a lot to be said for it. From then on, she was more than welcome.

❧

With spring, I grew restless. Getting out the long-neglected gig, which I kept at a black-owned livery stable on Canal Street, I polished it and made forays up and down Broadway, absorbing what my father had called the feel of the town. Then in May, remembering how she professed to be all a-squirm with roots and buds, I invited Thelma for an outing to the Park.

"You have a gig? I had no idea!"

"It's only a light two-wheeler. For the man about town; seats two. A folding top. If the weather's nice, we'll put it down."

"Junius, I've never been in a carriage in my life! And I've never seen the Park!"

No question, she was impressed. By switching with Julie, she thought she could get a Monday afternoon off.

"Next Monday, then."

"Yes, but don't come to the curb in front. I'll meet you at the corner."

"Why?"

"I don't know how Ida would feel about her help showing up at the brownstone in a carriage."

"It's just a gig."

"Even so."

"All right, I'll meet you at the corner at two."

❧

When I arrived at the corner, sporting my best topper, my plaid vest, and a fancy shirt adorned with my breast pin, I hardly recognized her. Waiting for me was a stylish young woman in a striped blue satin dress and a dotted veil, under the canopy of a parasol of fringed green silk. When I had helped her up and she sat right there beside me, I caught the trace of a fragrance from her dark hair under a velvet hat lined with blond lace. Here was a woman worthy of my brownstone. I was bedazed and bedazzled.

All up the Fifth Avenue she gaped at the fancy brownstones; I made sure to point out Restell's. Once on the Drive in the Park, she was amazed at the steady stream of turnouts thronged with parasoled belles and their top-hatted, frock-coated beaus. Casually I identified the different kinds of rig—phaeton, brougham, caleche—till her eyes grew round with wonder. In turn we saw the Pond, the Mall, the Lake, then the vast expanse of the Reservoir, flecked with silver ripples in the sun, and the North End's ravines and wooded knolls. The leaves were half out; birds were singing. Here and there the bough of a cherry or an apple tree had exploded in a blast of pink or white.

"Junius, it's so beautiful! I've never seen such greenery, or so much water touched by the sun! Eden must have been like this."

Coming back down from the North End, I pointed out black-faced sheep in a meadow, swans gliding on the Lake, an antlered buck and some does in an enclosure, and peacocks strutting near a walk, flashing green-gold tails in the sun. It was all new to her; she marveled. Finally we stopped in a grove and ate a picnic snack she had brought.

"Junius, this has been one of the most perfect days of my life. I thank you from the bottom of my heart."

"So, the schoolteacher's brat doesn't mind a bit of greenery?" I was hoping that she'd talk about herself at last.

"No, she doesn't. She's starved for it."

"Did your mother teach here in the city?"

"Yes, a little school on Bleecker Street. She had a way with children. She wanted me to teach there, too."

"You didn't?"

"No."

"What happened?"

"The riots. The school wasn't touched, but half the families who sent their children there left the city and never came back. And the others were afraid to let their children out of the house. The school closed, and something in Momma broke. She died within a year."

*Like Poppa*, I thought. "I'm sorry."

"So, I got a job as a maid, and then Julie told me about a position at Ida's. Ida puts on airs, I suppose, but she keeps it all from getting too vulgar. Even so, Momma must be turning over in her grave."

"You have no other family?"

"None."

I took her hand; she withdrew it.

"Junius, let's not spoil a day like this. Can we drive some more? It's paradise!"

I drove her again past the Lake and the Mall.

Late that evening I saw her in the hall. Again she thanked me profusely, and again I took her hand. By now I was pretty steamed up.

"No, Junius, please. It's been too perfect a day."

Saying that, she slipped into her room and shut the door.

Doors had been shut in my face too often. I had given her the ride of her life, and still she put me off. To hell with her grace and gentility! I was riled.

When my Visitant returned, I welcomed her in silence with a vengeance, stroked her soft hair gently as she pleasured me, then let her leave without any attempt at discovery. It became a delicious habit. Every few days—the exact timing was unpredictable—I had a fresh red rose to put in my vase. Now, who she was I didn't want to know. Owing me nothing, she gave me everything. Magical moments, rich and forbidden.

❧

On the outing with Thelma I thought I had recognized Lester in livery, sitting ramrod-stiff, arms folded, in the rumble seat of a passing carriage in the Park. So I wasn't too surprised when, one Monday evening, I bumped into him again on Broadway, his yellow topper just a bit frayed, his low-cut vest displaying a shirtfront devoid of a diamond, but with a carnation in his lapel of the kind often worn by grooms.

"Junius, how glorious it is to be back in this city! Here one breathes opportunity and finds diversions worthy of a lover of life."

"Things didn't work out down in Dixie?"

"For a while it was glorious. I was the Yankee slicker who dressed flash and hobnobbed with the assistant commissioner (so people thought; I didn't disabuse them) and all the local black politicians. The black folks called me 'Massa Hicks,' then 'Massa Lester,' and brought me gifts of live chickens and melons. And their womenfolk were generous, too. Down there I lived like a king."

"Then why did you leave?"

"The white folks hated my guts. I would have toughed it out, but the subassistant commissioner, who was a bit too fond of the grape, had his fingers in any number of pies. When charges of graft cropped up, I thought it prudent to decamp."

"Leaving your benighted brethren down South?"

"The hardy ones will find their way North. But what news of you? Still settled in your brownstone?"

"Yes, the one you pointed me to. But you didn't tell me it was a brothel."

"I didn't? But Junius, everyone knows of Madam Ida's!"

"You referred to her as Mrs. Ida Clayborn. How was I to know?"

"No matter, you've got your brownstone. Though I suppose it's a bit of a pinch, eyeing high-class tarts you mustn't touch."

"Most of them leave me cold. Too distant, too confected." I didn't mention my Doodlebug.

"In that case, I've heard of just the place for you—a rich, hot dose of life!"

Once again he dragged me off, this time to an Eighth Ward dive on Grand Street, where cobblestones were matted with garbage thrown from windows, and sidewalks reeked with trash. Standing at the entrance was a woman who looked like a huge black turtle rearing up on its hind legs, her lips a red gash, her hair in a yellow bandanna, her ears pierced by fake gold hoops. Seeing us, she flashed a smile.

"Welcome to Big Sue's, honeys. Come on in! We ain't elegant, but you'll have a bitchin' good time!"

Entering, we found ourselves in a cellar ill lit by kerosene lamps, with scraps of rag carpet on the floor, and windows stuffed with cardboard. To our nostrils came cheap perfumes and a muffled hint of old boot, green cheese. For a moment I felt like a naked diver in a grotto where eyes peered from crannies and lush flowers bloomed. The flowers were women; Big Sue talked them up.

"Gents, dis here is Fat Annie, she a big, thick puddin', try her. An' dis is Missy Lou, she a blonde dis mont', mebbe a redhead de next; she just a trickle o' honey. An' over dere by de window, dat sassy gal wid a perky pink fedder in her hair, dat am Liza Ann, she fancy as fur mittens. She sleeped wid aldermen, she sleeped wid de police chief hisself. You a sport, you right down her alley!"

Lester and I were the first customers of the evening; Sue waved us to a table. From behind a faded calico curtain she produced a cheap whiskey and glasses. Hardly had I taken my first sip and winced as it singed my throat, when the one called Liza Ann, wearing a low-cut bodice, a short tasseled skirt, and scarlet boots with jangly bells on the tops of them, plumped down on my lap.

"Hello, sport, ain't never seen you here before. Where you been keepin' yourself? Gonna give us girls a break, huh? How about a sip for Liza Ann?"

With that, she took a long gulp of my drink.

"Hey, that's supposed to be mine!" I half-protested.

"What's yours is mine, honey, and what's mine is yours. That way everybody's happy. Now put a quarter in my stocking for luck."

She hiked her skirt, exposing an expanse of warm brown flesh; I dropped a quarter in her stocking.

Meanwhile Missy Lou had similarly perched on Lester, who was grinning ear to ear, while under Fat Annie's cigar-thick fingers a piano plonked and tinkled. It was sleazy and cheap; I loved it.

I took a second swig, before Liza Ann could have another gulp; it burned.

"Say, what's this stuff you're serving? It tastes like kerosene."

"It's called 'benzine,' sugar," said Liza Ann. "It's a he-man's drink. Ain't you up to it?" She wiggled about on my lap, jangling her bells, and detected my erection. "Ooh, honey, you're all here tonight, ain't left nothin' at home. A lover boy for sure!" She plucked out her feather, tickled my nose with it. "How about comin' in back, give me a bit of your spunk? Since you're new here, I'll give you a special price: two bucks for a first-rate poke."

By now more customers had arrived, some black, some white. A black man was scraping a fiddle, and another one a bass fiddle, while Fat Annie drubbed the piano. Lester and Missy Lou were stomping and whirling to the music; at times he'd lift her high in the air, and she'd cry "Hoop-la!" and scream. I wanted to join them, but the walls had got just a bit tipsy, so I let Liza Ann lead me past the calico curtain to a small, drab room in back.

"There!" she said, shutting the door. "Now you and me can get down to business."

What happened after that I remember only vaguely. Money changed hands, clothes were shed. There were lots of whispered *honey*s and *sugar*s, and a lot of kissing and pumping and sweating, till finally I spent. "Time's up, honey!" she announced, and propelled me, more or less dressed, back toward the room in front. Lester and Missy Lou were gone; a crowd was singing and dancing. I stumbled to the door, heard a cheery "Come again, honey!" from Sue, and went home in a daze.

The next day my brain felt like someone had driven spikes deep into it; I had a foul taste in my mouth. It took all my concentration to get through my work of the day. Thelma noticed, said nothing, and that's how I wanted it. I hadn't been fuddled like this in years.

During the week I kept thinking of Liza Ann, her tasseled skirt, her boots with bells, her stinky perfume, the way she'd plumped down on my lap. She wasn't my first whore; I knew her for a cheap tart, as common as they come. Oddly enough, during that same week my Lady of the Rose stopped her visits. Had she tired of me? Had the hot weather got her down? I didn't brood about it, being fixed now on Liza Ann.

Of course I went back to Grand Street, this time without Lester.

"Hi dere, Young America, welcome back!" said Sue, her hair in a green scarf, gold hoops dangling from her ears; she waved me in again. "Black folks o' white folks, if dey got de money, everybody's welcome heah. Who else in de city say *dat*?"

Inside, the same dingy den, the smells of boot and cheese, five girls, three customers.

"Lover boy!" cried Liza Ann, gaudy in another short skirt with tassels, who darted over to me, boots jangling, and again sat on my lap.

"Come back to Liza Ann, didn't you, sugar? 'Cause you know what's good. I'm the honey pot of this outfit, I'm the rub with a tickle. So, how you doin' tonight?"

"Okay, I guess." It was easier to let her do the talking.

Just then Sue came back in with a bluecoat, his silver shield glinting in the half-light, and delivered up to him a young white customer in elegant but rumpled clothes who was obviously deep in his cups.

"Heah, officer, heah's de article hisself, an' heah's de hunert-dollah bill he wants to pay wid. How I change a hunert-dollah bill? Ain't no one in de neighborhood wid change like dat. You see him safe outa heah, all right? Ain't nobody gonna get me closed for thievin'!"

The drunk stumbled out in the gentle custody of the Law. Everyone agreed that in Sue the Turtle's house no customer ever got robbed.

After a quick glass of "benzine," I found myself in the back room again with Liza Ann, but this time the walls weren't so tipsy.

"Another dollar, sport. My rates have gone up, 'cause I'm in hot demand!"

I grumbled, paid.

"All right now, sport. We gonna climb the mountain."

She kissed me; we undressed. Soon we were locked together, her legs twisting snakelike into mine, and I was pumping and pumping, till suddenly I'd spent like never in my life, and she had got there, too, and for a few moments I coasted on the joy of it. Finally, gently, I got out of her and we lay there side by side, coming down slowly together, and I drifted and dozed and almost fell asleep.

"Time's up, lover boy! Up and out!"

Her voice stabbed me; I twitched, opened my eyes. She was over by a wash basin, rubbing herself with a cloth.

"Hey, what are you doing?"

"Washin' your muck outa me. I've got another customer waitin'."

"It's not muck."

"Hell it ain't!"

This jarred me, for I'd always thought of my spunk as something precious. Once I'd dressed, I took hold of her to kiss her.

"Wanna swap spit? You're crazy."

She laughed, kissed me, and shoved me out the door.

As I was leaving, a party of silk-hatted gentlemen arrived; I lingered, watched. Among them was Justice George G. Barnard, white topper and all, who within minutes had Missy Lou perched on his lap. Like me, he craved the depths. When our eyes met briefly, he gave no sign of recognition, nor did I.

# 17

SHE WAS BECOMING A BAD HABIT. *THE WRONG OBSESsion,* I told myself. *What has she to do with my brownstone?* True enough: once I crossed the magic threshold of a brownstone and became a part of its sumptuous interior, women outside it lost their appeal for me, seemed coarse and drab. Yet here I was, panting after the crudest of whores. During the week I kept thinking of her jangling bells, her silly feather, her warm flesh. I had dreams of being in a garden where tight buds opened into huge deep-throated flowers crawling with ants and worms that swarmed all over me into my groin, mouth, and eyes, while the brown muck pulsed with life. Then I woke up, rock-hard, and wanted her.

If the Paradigms of Vice and Virtue had any validity at all, I was trapped in the den called Lust, just this side of Murder and the corpse-dangling gallows of the prison, well on my way to hell. But I knew that hell was not out there; it was deep inside me.

Tuesday was Thelma's day off, so before I retired in the evening it was understood that I would knock on Ida's bedroom door and ask if she needed anything. Usually she didn't, but one night she said, "Come in."

She was sitting in a rocking chair near the monumental bed, a half-empty glass of sherry on a side table, the gaslight low. I approached her, waited.

"Junius, could you place that bandbox on top of the wardrobe?"

I did as requested. The box was light; she could easily have lifted it herself. Again, I waited. Fanning herself, she rocked gently, spoke softly without looking at me.

"Junius, I was a banker's daughter, a giddy young thing, quite headstrong, spoiled, wedged too tight in virtue. At seventeen I ran off with a dapper salesman sporting a red vest and a smile who said I was the light of his life. In time he got bored and deserted me."

As she talked on, I remained silent. She wanted a listener, nothing more.

"My next lover was a gambler, a tall, sinister man, quite handsome. Before or after he would clasp my throat and tell me, 'I could kill you with just one little squeeze.' I was bound to him through passion spiced with fear. Knowing this, he nudged me into whoredom, said he needed money to pay debts, I must do this to prove my love. Thanks to him, I learned all about men, their sweaty bodies, their strange, savage needs."

I still listened quietly, waiting for her to continue.

"He kept the money I gave him in a little silver box on his bureau. He was so sure of me, he never locked the box or hid it. Over time my love turned to hate. One morning when he was sleeping late in a drunken stupor, I quietly packed up all my best things and left, taking with me his gold studs and tiepin and the silver box. I still have great pleasure imagining his shock, then fury, on waking, but by then I was miles away. After that I continued on my own, studied men for years, learned what they wanted, or thought they wanted, and determined to provide it—on my own terms, at a price."

She paused, resumed, a hard tone in her voice.

"Junius, most men are crude, selfish, deceitful, often childish, disgusting, and in all but practical matters, stupid. They look ridiculous in their drawers, are too timid or too brash. Thank God, I can leave them now to my girls. I am repelled by hairy hands and thighs. I loathe the smell of semen."

Never had I heard her talk like this; I was astonished.

She took another sip of sherry. "Thank you, Junius. You may go."

I tiptoed out, softly closed the door. As I went, I noticed a small silver box on her bureau.

Back in my own room, I pondered. I knew that Thelma had never heard these confidences, suspected that I was the first one ever to receive them. Why me? I had no idea.

Though I was keeping a distance between me and Thelma, I told her of Ida's revelations. She too was surprised.

"So, it's the same story as with the girls. Almost always, there's a man or men involved. I knew she hated them, but until now I didn't know why."

"But why tell *me*, a man?"

"You're black. You don't count."

"But I *do* count. She's singled me out."

"She trusts you. If she told a woman, she'd feel she was losing control. Ida has to have control."

"I still don't get it."

"Neither do I."

❧

The sticky hot weather had come; I sweated, slept naked. There were fewer callers; they were taking their families out of town or traveling in Europe. But I was constantly on edge, cool to Thelma, short-tempered with Philip and Dennis, and so harsh to Julie in overseeing her work that I almost reduced her to tears:

"Oh Junius, I try so hard. I do, I really do!"

When I tried to read in my room, my mind fuzzed, and I thought of Liza Ann. Often I ended up staring at my latest spoil from the cellar storeroom, which I had placed on a windowsill. It was a long-stemmed ruby glass called (so Thelma told me) a luster, with a floral design in gold and a bowl-shaped top from which hung little cut-glass prisms that broke up the light from the window and cast a rainbow all over the room. If I touched the glass drops ever so slightly, they trembled, making flecks of blue, green, yellow, and red dance over the ceiling and walls. Watching this play of colors took my mind off the den on Grand Street—for a while.

When I went back, Liza Ann was dancing with a white man.

"You'll have to wait your turn, Junior. Got a he-man here who's promised me the frig of my life!"

While I was waiting, shouts erupted from behind the calico curtain, and Missy Lou emerged in a frilly pink dress, blonde wig askew, followed by a man wrapped only in a sheet.

"He's crazy!" she yelled. "He's crazy!"

"Bitch!" cried the client. "You copped my wallet!"

"What do I know about his wallet?"

Sue waddled over, plunged her hand down Missy Lou's bosom, yanked out a wallet, and went at her with a voice like a hacking knife.

"You little squeak of a tart, you string bean in itchy un'erwear flauntin' round wid yo' piss-yellow hair, you a shame to me! Black folks don't go totin' t'ings off—white trash do dat. You fixin' to get me closed? Move, Missy. I catch you, I claw you bald!"

Lunging in undulant rage, she chased Missy Lou out the door, ripping from the girl pink frills and tufts of yellow hair, their shouts so loud the whole block heard. With fanfare the wallet was returned to the sheet-clad client. On Grand Street Missy Lou was never seen again.

In my session with Liza Ann that followed, I spent gloriously, but sensed that, for all her gasps and moans, she was faking.

"That's it, Junior. Time's up!"

She had taken to calling me Junior instead of Junius, and often, when I kissed her, emitted a shrill laugh that grated on my nerves. I knew I was being played for a fool, but couldn't help it; she was in my blood and bone.

"Come in, Junius," said Ida, when I knocked on her door that Tuesday night.

Again she was sitting in the rocking chair, rocking gently and fanning herself, a glass of sherry on the table. This time she had no pretext of a task to assign me. I stood near, just out of her sight.

"Junius, I grew up in a big house in a small town upstate. One day, when I am rich, old, and tired enough, I shall retreat up there to a town just like it and buy a mansion on a deep, smooth lawn sloping down to an avenue shaded by maples. The house will have a wide front porch, bay windows and cupolas and turrets, many rooms, grounds with trees and shrubs. There I shall receive lady friends and give to politicians and the poor. Under clean white ceilings, in dry hours of respectability I shall read Voltaire, Hume, Kant. It would be reassuring to understand this strange game, this frantic grinding of the senses. Perhaps, in time, some meaning will emerge. You will of course accompany me."

"Ma'am, I don't know if that will be possible."

"Of course it will. I need you."

With that, she waved me away.

Once again I pondered in my room. She hadn't asked me, she had told me. There was a hardness about her that put me off. Yet for the first time it occurred to me that this woman might need me more than I needed her. Did this give me power? The upstate mansion: in my fertile mind, the germ of a new fantasy.

❧

When I next went to Sue's, Liza Ann, gaudy and jangly as ever, was partying with others; she told me again I'd have to wait my turn. Then Fat Annie whispered to me, "Sue's down. Cheer her up."

Sue was sitting in a corner by herself, far from the noise of the partying. I went and sat beside her. It was the first time I'd seen her in her cups. She took no notice of me, stared at the drink in her hand.

"Junius," she finally said, "I'se fat, I'se ugly. Men don't want me. I miss dat ol' Long Tom."

As with Ida, I knew to just listen.

"Look what dey done in de riots."

She raised her sleeve, showed her whole arm hatched with scars. I winced at the sight of it.

"Dere was a big mob of screamin' Irish women. Dey burst into my den, stripped my girls, who fled buff naked down de street. Den dey stripped me too, beat an' stomped me, an' drank up all my booze. While dey was tankin' up, I staggered off, bleedin' from cuts all over. Friends took me in an' salved me, gave me some cloze. Over an' over I sobbed, 'Dey ain't got no right!' Den, when t'ings calmed down again, I come back here, swept an' scrubbed, an' opened up again. Guts, folks said. Hell, it's de only t'ing I know how to do."

Her face was racked with pain.

*"Dey ain't got no right!"*

She had yelled so loud, the whole room stared. Then, more softly:

"Last time dey come for de booze. Next time dey come for me. Wid spikes, knives. Dey gonna cut me up."

She stared off into space, seemed almost to hear the murmurs of a mob. I shivered; I almost heard them, too. Then she twitched, as if shaking free from a nightmare.

"It's a mean world, but I ain't played out yet."

She fell silent, stared into space.

Sue had unsettled me. I was still unsettled, when Liza Ann fetched me back to her room, which smelled, I now realized, of sweat, semen, cheap perfume, and mold.

"All right, little boy, time for your lollipop, ain't it?"

With effort I got it off with her, but this was a quick-and-dirty, she didn't even bother to fake. I was angry.

"That's it, Junior. Time's up!"

She had called me Junior once too often. Springing to my feet, I slapped her so hard that she went reeling across the room, hit the wall, and slumped down on the floor. She cowered there, speechless, astonished, registering a real look of fear. I dressed quickly, strode over to her, spat, walked out.

All the way home I was exultant: *Rid of the bitch at last!* My excitement masked a smoldering inside me. By the time I got back, I was feverish; head burning, I fell naked into bed.

# 18

TOSSING IN A FEVER, I SLEPT, WOKE, SLEPT, LOST ALL track of time. Chandeliers glittered, voices recited "Tears, Idle Tears," a commode broached from the sea like a dolphin, and a busty bronze Venus flowed into a torrent of mother-of-pearl and tortoiseshell fans. I groaned, writhed in sweaty sheets. "I be come to heal you" was whispered in my ear, and bulbs of garlic were hung, while the white and black keys of a pianoforte plonked and tinkled on their own, and a voice chanted "Junior junior junior . . . hell it ain't!" Then someone put cool cloths to my brow, and I smelled cherry blossoms and lilac. Looming beside me, a huge four-poster bed with silk damask hangings dissolved, and a flashing constellation of jewels melted into a thick brown muck that ran off in rivulets and vanished.

I opened my eyes: Thelma.

"You're better now. The fever has subsided."

I sat up, looked around. Light was streaming through a window, to be broken by the pendants of the luster into a play of rainbows. A huge vase held pink and yellow roses; a canary sang.

"How long have I been sick?"

"Two days. We've been worried about you."

Over the bed hung bulbs of garlic.

"Garlic. Did you . . . ?"

"Yes, I hung it up. Something I learned from my mother. Always good for a fever."

"Then you're the one who told me, 'I be come to heal you'?"

"No, never. I'm not a healer. I just know a few things from Momma."

"Well, someone said it."

"You've been hallucinating."

"Did anyone put cool cloths to my forehead?"

"Me and Julie; we spelled each other out. Dennis brought the flowers from the garden."

"And the canary?"

"Ida. To cheer you up."

"*She* was here?"

"Several times. We were worried, so we all looked in."

"She saw the room, with all the stuff from the storeroom?"

"Of course."

"What did she say?"

"Nothing."

"Nothing at all?"

"Nothing at all. She wants you to get well. We all do. This place isn't the same without you."

I was weak and fevered out, had trouble absorbing it all. She took my hand.

"You've been a long way off, Junius, but now I hope you're back. I was unkind to you before; I'm sorry. I was hurt once, hurt bad, so I'm afraid of being hurt again. Be patient with me, please. Be kind."

My anger at her had died down, disappeared. "Tell me," I said.

"An older man, a friend of my mother's. I was a bit giddy; he was more in love with himself than with me."

A rare confidence. "Tell me more."

"I'd rather not. Not much to tell, anyway. What's done is done. At least I learned from it. I learned a lot."

A silence. I knew not to ask any more. Finally I spoke.

"I owe you all an apology."

"For being sick?"

"For being nasty and selfish and mean. But maybe that's all burned out of me. Yes, I've been a long way off, but I'm back."

"Rest now. Don't try to get up. Marie will send up a broth when you're hungry. One of us will look in from time to time."

She left. I was being bathed in kindness, far more than I deserved. I sank back on the pillow. In my strayings to Grand Street I had betrayed Thelma, my brownstone, and myself. The canary sang, the roses breathed their freshness, and rainbows danced over the ceiling and walls. Would all this be enough to cure me of self-disgust? Suddenly, feeling nauseous, I lurched up from the bed, staggered to the bathroom, sank to my knees, and vomited into the commode. Weak, dazed, I stumbled back to bed, fell into it, and slept.

Two days later I was able to resume my duties, albeit gingerly. I returned the canary to the parlor, thanked Dennis for the roses, Marie for the broth, and Julie, Thelma, and Ida for their attentions, and apologized for any recent sharpness or discourtesy. All were gracious, and Julie announced again with a smile, "Oh Junius, I just drink up kindness." Even the china dolls, though more distant, seemed glad to see me up and about. From Ida, no comment about my furnishings borrowed from the storeroom. And when, a week later, I dropped in on Bessie and Dilly, whom I had long neglected, they hailed the return of the prodigal.

"Junius," said Bessie, "you been sick."

"Yes, Aunt Bessie, but I'm over it."

"Maybe, maybe not. You look peaked. Don't he look peaked, Dilly?"

"Yes he do. Plumb beat out, I'd say."

So, they sat me down and fixed me up a savory soup like nothing I'd ever tasted in my life. Whatever went into it, I knew it was seasoned with love.

In the Paradigms of Vice and Virtue I recalled a Slough of Self-Disgust, but no path leading from it to the Vale of Loving Forgiveness, where I was now recuperating. Did I deserve this kindness? For weeks to come, in bed at night I heard Liza Ann's shrill laugh and taunts, smelled her perfume and the mingled sweat of our bodies, felt a hint of nausea.

❧

With September came cooler weather and the return of many of the regulars to the city; business picked up. Night after night I watched in fascination, as Ida flashed her most engaging smile at these patrons she so loathed. One evening when the parlor was crowded with callers, she motioned me over and whispered, "Those two gentlemen at the far end of the parlor require minimal refreshment and will certainly not be going upstairs. No matter; please extend them every courtesy."

I nodded but was puzzled. Ida's visitors were expected to spend at least a hundred dollars per visit, and the two in question, sitting apart, showed little sign of doing so. One was a crisp old man in pinstripes, his eyes popping as he surveyed the scene and frantically scribbled notes. The other, a stocky man with a handlebar mustache, sat quietly, occasionally exchanging words with his companion, but otherwise detached. For refreshment they ordered soda water—unheard of at Ida's—and were ceremoniously served with the same. At one point I heard the older man say, more to himself than his companion, "A bitter, bitter brew. Would that this chalice could be taken from my lips." Wary-eyed, he certainly wasn't talking about the soda water. After an hour they left.

"The elderly gentleman," Ida then explained to me, "is a well-known and highly respected minister of the Gospel from Connecticut. He visits us every year or two, purporting to gather notes for his sermons, which depict the city as Satan's Empire, Sodom, Gomorrah, and the New Babylon all rolled into one. It does no harm. In fact, his rantings bring us business."

"And the other one?"

"Mr. Blake, a city detective with whom I am acquainted. He escorts him through dens of iniquity."

A reminder of Ida's mysterious arrangements with the police. As for sinks of sin, I would gladly have directed the reverend to Grand Street and Liza Ann; vivid sermons would certainly result.

That was not the only incursion of morality. Every month for close to two years Ida had been receiving an injunction to repentance on beige paper in a delicate hand "from one who loves Jesus." Shrugging, she had numbered each (twenty-three to date) and dropped it in an onyx box on her writing desk in the library. One day I presented her with the calling card of two ladies of the Female Reform Society who had asked to see her. To my surprise, Ida told me to show them in.

Confronting Ida in the library were two ladies of a certain age, one tall and skinny, one squat and plump, sleeved to the knuckles and buttoned to the chin. I stood just inside the door and watched.

"Dearest sister," said the tall one, "we come to you in a spirit of compassion. For the sake of purity . . ."

". . . the city's good name . . ." said the squat one.

". . . and your immortal soul, we beg you . . ."

". . . we implore you . . ."

". . . to reform."

Ida smiled. "Your society serves many worthy goals, I assume?"

"Oh yes," said the tall one. "We are called into the hedges and byways."

"There," said the squat one, "we visit prisons and almshouses and haunts of degradation."

Without another word, Ida sat at her desk and wrote.

"This," she said, handing something to the tall one, "is a check for one thousand dollars, to further the society's good works. I wish you the best."

Hesitant, the tall one took it.

"Bertha, how can you?" gasped the squat one, who snatched the check and thrust it back at Ida.

A whispered disputation ensued, watched by Ida with a faint smile, following which the two ladies abruptly withdrew. I saw them to the door. At last glimpse, they were descending the stoop in heated argument. No beige note ever came again.

Only as bitter memories of Liza Ann faded, and with them my sense of shame and guilt, did I start seeing Thelma again. Without her, my possession of the brownstone would never be complete. I resolved to court her discreetly, so as to gain her trust. One brisk autumn day I took her in my gig to the Battery. As we went down Broadway in the crunch of vehicles, she marveled at the carts and stages and carriages all jumbled up together and dashing so furiously that no pedestrian dared venture in the street. At the Battery I tethered my horse and we strolled on the promenade, enjoying a fine view of the river and the harbor. Tall-masted sailing vessels passed in the distance, stubby ferries plied back and forth, sleek sidewheelers glided by, and small craft bobbed and darted in their wakes. For Thelma, this was all new; she had rarely glimpsed the harbor.

Having at times strolled along the waterfront, I could tell her how the Jersey City ferries carried thousands of passengers daily, cracking through twelve-inch ice in the winter. I told her how the packets from Havre and Liverpool brought in gold and ivory and silks and wines, and how shipyards echoed with clanging hammers and screeching saws, rearing up skeletons of hulls. I described how brownstone from New Jersey and Connecticut was unloaded here. I even told her how once a day the offal boat set off up the river, its deck piled high with the smelly carcasses of horses, cows, pigs, dogs, and cats removed from the streets, to be delivered to a bone-boiling plant up the river that would turn them into leather, glue, and soap. Was ever a woman so wooed, with tales of screeching saws and dead pigs and glue? The china dolls would have shrunk from it all in horror; she relished it.

"This is what drives the city," I explained. "Trade is its life's blood. It's where brownstone luxury comes from."

"You love this city, don't you?"

"It's not a city easy to love, least of all if you're black. But yes, I guess I do. It's Go Ahead."

But after contemplating this orgy of bustle and noise, echoed in the traffic of Broadway, we were both glad to return to the quiet of a brownstone, with its charmed interiors.

In those interiors once again I nourished fantasies of Thelma giving herself at last amid marble, gilt, and brocade, with smells of polished oak and black walnut, and scented candles and lilac and pine. These fantasies brought balm to my brain, joy to my heart, and peace to my doodle: the fulfillment of my most grandiose ambition and my deepest need.

❧

Not that my doodle had been neglected. As the cooler weather came, my Visitant returned, wordlessly pleasuring me and leaving a red rose on my pillow. Being immersed again in fantasies of Thelma, I felt I had to end these visits, though I wasn't sure how. Finally I told Thelma, saying only that an unknown woman had slipped into my room uninvited. I omitted the graphic details, how I'd delighted in it, and how long this had been going on. She was amazed.

"You have no clue at all who it was?"

"None."

"This is serious. The butler before you got caught with one of the girls in his room. Ida got rid of them both on the spot."

This I hadn't known. "But I didn't ask her in."

"Who except me would believe you? Will she come again?"

"Maybe. Probably."

"You've got to keep her out."

"How can I? The door has no latch."

"Put some furniture against it at night. If she can't sneak in quietly, she'll probably give it up."

I did as Thelma suggested, shoving my armchair against the door. It might not hold, but if someone pressed against it, the bumps and scrapes would wake me up. After that, once or twice in the middle of the night I heard—or thought I heard—a faint noise at the door, but no one pushed it open. For a whole month I kept the chair smack against the door at night.

What a situation: fighting off a whore in a whorehouse! Lester would have roared. But I now realized that my continued presence in the brownstone—the very dream I was living—was threatened by my Lady of the Rose. A white woman seeking out a black man to commit delicious acts of sodomy: we were breaking every rule in the books, both Ida's and society's. However magical, these visits had to stop. Finally they did. Farewell my Doodlebug, my Wanton.

❧

"Hello there, ladies and gents, good evenin' all, George Washington Jefferson Burns (quite a mouthful, ain't it?) at your service. Wash to some friends, Jeff to others, 'cause to me it don't matter a cat's miao. Vice President of the Peoria & Pacific Railroad—V.P., P.P.R. (has a nice ring, don't you think?). Glad indeed to be here, so how about champagne for all?"

Jaunty in checkered trousers with a jutting chin and beard, his mustache greased and twisted, he strode in like a conqueror, so crass and loud that I thought Ida would have me show him to the door. Maybe she was too taken aback, like the rest of us; in any case, she didn't. Every eye in the room was on him, as he passed out engraved cards right and left in the parlor. Even I, standing in the doorway, got one.

**George Washington Jefferson Burns**
**Vice President**
**Peoria & Pacific Railroad**
**82 Broadway, New York City**
**Destiny: The Eyes of the World Are Upon You**

"Honored I am to be here," Mr. Wash Burns continued. "Even in Peoria they've heard of Madame Ida's, and I must say, at first peep, it lives up to expectation. I know class, when I see it. So, here's to Madame Ida and her lovely team of fillies, the pride and grace of Gotham!"

By now, Philip and Thelma were scurrying to hand out glasses of champagne. The gentlemen present lifted their glasses to the ladies, who couldn't help but smile.

"Ladies and gents, I'm here on a mission. The first transcontinental railroad is now almost not a dream but a fact. This great continent of ours is bein' spanned by twin bright bands of steel sprintin' over plains past buffalo and astonished Injuns, across mile-deep canyons on trestlework, up and down piney mountains into the sunny clime of Californiay, its rugged shorelands washed by the blue Pacific. Beyond that vast expanse of water lurks the final, the most ultimate mystery, the Orient. These is wondrous times!"

His voice pealed, his eyes shone like lanterns in the dark. They were all sipping bubbly and listening; he had us in the palm of his hand.

"Ladies and gents, out there in our rambunctious West there's a great-rivered continent sculpted by the Almighty, with prairies just beggin' to be settled, mountains burstin' with ore, and cattle-teemin' towns waitin', prayin' for a railroad: the Union Pacific, the Northern Pacific, the Atlantic & Pacific, and the Peoria & Pacific, of which I'm honored to be the vice president. This very minute, out there in the goodlands of the West, history is bein' made!"

That Madam Ida would let her parlor become a broker's front office, touting the prospects of the Peoria & Pacific Railroad, amazed me, but she seemed to be enthralled by this charmer. So were the china dolls and their admirers without exception, and to some extent myself. His words sparked us, made us see booted surveyors with instruments mapping buttes and hillocks, made us hear spades click, axes hew, and blasts lop sides of mountains. He made us almost touch gold in gulches, silver-laced crags, and freighted tonnages of ore. Suddenly we believed in pistoned miracles, in getting rich under the hand of Providence, in space and time obliterated, the continent, the world made one by links of steel.

"Yes, there are nay-sayers," Mr. Wash Burns conceded. "They talk about grasshopper plagues that eat up crops, harnesses, and window curtains. They talk about town sites marked by a buffalo skull and little else, and parched mesas whose Injuns, buffalo, and rattlesnakes voice no need of a railroad. What do I say to them? I say, folks, this railroad of mine is the goin'est scheme around, puttin' tracks through a privilege of country. It's for big-brained men—and women—and that's the nuts and the bolts of it. Investors will make millions. I say, *Destiny.* I say, *Progress.* Westward ho, folks, westward ho!"

When, at this point, Mr. Wash produced a long sheet of paper and a gold-tipped pen and invited subscriptions for stock, several of the gentlemen callers, their minds wrenched from lechery, flocked around him, eager to sign. Two of the china dolls did also, and the rest looked on with interest, as if at least half convinced. I myself had to curb an impulse to do so.

Having secured a bounty of names, Mr. Wash proposed another toast: "To the riches of Wyomin' and Colorado! To the green, fertile fields of Nevada! To the forests of Utah! To hope! To energy! To progress!"

Clinking all the glasses within reach, he drank, and so did they all. Then, almost as an afterthought, some of the gentlemen—and Mr. Wash, too—turned their attention to the ladies, with whom they began to pair off. Conversations followed, Mr. Wash's the loudest by far, punctuated with bursts of laughter, mostly his own. Even after he went upstairs with Doris of the spit curls, in the parlor his words seemed to pulse in the air; you could almost hear *energy* and *hope*.

# 19

From then on, Mr. Wash was all over the place. He became a regular at Madam Ida's, a great favorite with the girls and the staff. He called us by name, tipped well, joked, winked, guffawed, and spieled on about his railroad and the West.

"Junius," Thelma confided one day, "I have a little money set aside. Would Mr. Wash's railroad be a good investment?"

"I'd hold off. The Union Pacific will be completed next year, but all these other schemes are just plans and little else. When that man talks, he mixes his railroad up with the U.P. to the point where you can't tell the two apart."

"Where is Peoria, anyway? In Ohio?"

"No, I think in Iowa. Be that as it may, I'd wait."

So, Thelma did not invest.

But imagine my surprise when, a few days later, I noticed on Ida's desk in the library a stack of certificates tied in red tape. She being out of the room, I took a close look. Sure enough, stock certificates of the Peoria & Pacific Railroad, beautifully engraved on the finest paper, picturing a bosomy bunting-clad America (rather like the china dolls, I thought) throned atop a mountain of gold, with locomotives chugging across an expanse of prairie in the distance. At the bottom was the bold, fancy signature of G. Washington Burns, vice president. Knowing Madam Ida to be a shrewd businesswoman, I was impressed.

Next, taking Thelma to see the autumn foliage in the Park, I glimpsed Mr. Wash squiring his lady in a glossy phaeton, a light, open carriage with the top down, its thin wheels racing on the Drive. His checkered trousers were unmistakable and his chin jutting, as he grinned from the depths of his beard. As for Mrs. Wash, sprinkled all over with diamonds, her auburn hair ablaze in the sun, she looked like a force to be reckoned with.

"Don't they make a show!" I said to Thelma.

"Yes . . . but shoddy."

*Shoddy:* Mrs. Hammond's word for the New Money folks getting rich in the war. She had used it with the utmost scorn.

❧

That Mr. Wash's interests were wide-ranging became apparent one evening at Madam Ida's when, well out of the earshot of the hostess, he regaled a number of gentlemen with an account of Sue the Turtle. Recently Sue had received two ladies of the Female Reform Society who braved her cellar's old-boot smell to urge her to repent.

"Ladies, I just paid half my earnin's to de landlord, de roundsman, de captain, and de local t'ugs. Ladies, oh ladies, ain't no place worse dan heah. I'se goin' to hell wid bells on!"

He had Sue down to a T.

❧

I hadn't seen Lester since the evening he took me to Big Sue's. Remembering his frayed topper and gemless shirtfront, I assumed that by now he might well be shining shoes or posing as a maimed veteran to peddle pencils on Broadway. It was indeed on Broadway that I met him, but he was dressed in the height of fashion: a tweed sack coat and trousers with braiding down the side, a natty felt bowler, and a tasseled walking stick. He outshone me by far.

After the usual effusive greeting, he whisked me by stage down to Wall Street, where he informed me that the nation's destiny was unfolding. I'd never been there, thinking finance a white folks' game and no concern of mine. "Wall Street," he announced, "is a fountain of gold, if you know which spigots to turn."

What he showed me there were rows of temple-like banks and brokerage offices. The sidewalks were jammed with messengers carrying bags of coin and greenbacks, screaming newsboys, and ranting preachers. He pointed out the Stock Exchange, the Gold Room, the Custom House, and a noisy jam of top-hatted brokers trading stocks outside on the street. For me, it was a muddle.

"This is where fortunes are made or lost in a day," Lester expounded. "The purse strings of the nation, the keystone of the Union. Here, great ideas are hatched and financed." (As he spoke, I noticed a fat hog scrounging in the gutter.) "Money raised here will send railroads ever westward, twin bright bands of steel sprinting over plains past bison and astonished Indians, to bind a great-rivered continent—"

"Sculpted by the Almighty," I interposed. "And prairies just begging to be settled."

He stopped in mid-spiel, taken aback.

"Lester, are you working for Mr. G. Washington Burns, vice president of the Peoria & Pacific Railroad?"

"How did you know?"

"I recognize the rant."

Lester, it turned out, had been in Mr. Wash's employ for over a year, starting as groom and getting himself promoted to valet. He now attended Mr. Wash intimately, laying out his togs for the day, shining his boots and shoes, polishing his studs, and brushing his coat and sleek silk hat. In the course of these duties he had gleaned from his employer useful insights into the world of finance, to the point of making modest investments through Mr. Wash's broker, with astonishing results. Lester had become, to his knowledge and mine, the first black investor on Wall Street. As we strolled there I had noticed, with the exception of a peddler or two, not one black face in the crowd.

I explained to Lester my own connection with Mr. Wash, including his account of Sue the Turtle, so as to discourage Lester from further visits to Grand Street, since it would be mutually awkward, should he and his boss meet while cavorting there. And when Lester began to talk up Mr. Wash's railroad as the "goin'est scheme around," I respectfully declined to buy stock.

"These are flash times," Lester announced. "The men are flash, the women are flash, the carriages are flash. Flash ideas are begetting flash schemes. It's all cancans and champagne. Don't stay in a corner, Junius. You'll miss the time of your life!"

We parted, promising to keep in touch. Admittedly, Lester's touting of Flash had affected me. I decided that my shoes weren't shined enough, my breast pin didn't gleam enough, I lacked glittery rings and studs. If these were flash times, I was damn well going to be flash!

Dressing flash was easy. On outings I donned a white waistcoat with coral studs over a pinstriped shirt, a gold watch fob, checkered trousers, and pearl-gray gloves. It took most of my savings to do it, but success was confirmed when Dilly exclaimed at the sight of me, "Ooh, Junius, you dress so flash!"

When I went out, Flash was all around me. In the windows of Tiffany's on Broadway, I could survey the jeweled fans and clocks, silver loving cups, and half-draped nymphs in bronze that were the gewgaws of Flash. And in the Park I saw, in the carriages on the Drive, the pageant and parade of Flash: railroad men and money barons and patent medicine kings with their wives, and Madame Restell in stylish finery, with her coachman in red and gold.

And Ida herself, whether sallying forth by carriage to deposit her earnings in the bank, or presiding over her parlor, her eagle-feather fan grazing her armament of jewels, wasn't she the epitome of Flash? Wasn't her parlor prodigiously flash? And its visitors, whom I had seen at my father's barbershop—them or their fathers or grandfathers—and again at Downing's, and again, a choice few, at Big Sue's: weren't they the high muckamucks of Flash? And hadn't I known them for ages, even before Flash was invented?

Lester had persuaded me to entrust him with a small amount of my savings, to be invested through Mr. Wash's broker in what Lester described as a "very flash stock." To my amazement, two weeks later he repaid me threefold, crediting a "nice little jump in the market." With this money in my pocket, dressed elegantly, I went again to Tiffany's on Broadway to gaze at their windows' glittering display. I wanted to buy Thelma some gaudy little bauble, some trinket that was dazzlingly flash. Tiffany's imposing façade, with its arches and monumental clock, deterred me: surely I couldn't afford their prices. Down the street I found what looked to be a modest little shop, its window flaunting jeweled fans, bronze statuettes, and tiny silver vases. I went in to price the fans.

Immediately a clerk scurried over: "The service entrance is next door."

"I don't want the service entrance," I announced. "I want to price some objects in the window."

"The service entrance is next door," he repeated, louder.

"I want to price some objects," I insisted.

By now every eye in the shop—customers and clerks alike—was on me. A mustached older man who looked like the manager came over:

*"The service entrance is next door!"*

He had all but shouted. At last I got the message. Seething with rage and shame, I curbed the urge to pommel him, spun about, stalked out.

Striding the pavement, I raged, as angry with myself as with them. *Fool! Fool! Fool! Just because you have a little money and are dressed to the nines, do you think that you, a black man, can enter a fancy Broadway shop? Have you learned nothing in all these years? Flash is a party for whites. You, you fool, aren't invited!*

My fury mounting, I went back to the little shop; through the window I saw the clerks fussing over customers as if nothing had happened, while passersby strode past, oblivious of my rage. Suddenly I saw a loose brick in the gutter. I felt a great urge to hurl that brick through the little shop's window, and through the dazzling windows of Tiffany's, and all the fancy stores on the street. I wanted to smash up Delmonico's, that temple of exquisite dining, where the white elite feasted in an atmosphere that was said to be tastefully, discreetly, flash. And Fisk's Opera House, a marble palace with frescoed ceilings and crystal chandeliers, whose on-stage waterfalls and rousing cancans—bawdily, gaudily flash—I would never be privileged to view. A flash city, but I was locked out. Before I knew it, I had grabbed the brick and hurled it with great force at the window. It shattered, and for an instant I exulted in the big, jagged hole, the dirty brick lodged among the polished statuettes and vases, and the astonishment of all inside. Then, as a crowd started gathering, I strode off and got out of there fast.

By the time I got back to Ida's I had calmed down, even to the point of looking warily around me to make sure I hadn't been followed. The moment I saw Thelma in the hall, I blurted the whole story out.

"You're crazy!" she exclaimed, motioning me into the linen closet, where we could talk unobserved.

"They had it coming!"

At the thought of the havoc I had wrought, I felt the wildest joy. Something long held down inside me had at last got free.

"All right, they had it coming," said Thelma. "A lot of good that will do you, if they lock you up in jail!"

"The service entrance! I'm tired of being looked on as a servant! I'm tired of being Ida's flunkey! That's all I am, a flunkey!"

"Some flunkey! You run this brownstone. You decide who gets in and who doesn't. The clients are afraid of you, and so are the girls."

"So what? Thelma, have you ever heard of Buck Himes?"

"No. Who is he?"

"A living legend in the Five Points. An angry man, and tough. In his younger days he and his friends got drunk and bashed one another, and if the police came, they bashed the police. He lives in a stinking cellar on a blind alley in the Five Points, but he's happy there. 'No white man bosses me,' he boasts, 'and no black man either. I'm *free!'* And he is. He's never worked for white folks and scorns all those who do. When the riots came, he was ready behind his barricaded door with clubs and knives and rage. Word got around; they left him alone. Now *that's* what I call freedom!"

"How does he support himself?"

"There's always been some woman, black or white, living with him. He sends them out as hot corn girls, or ragpickers, or dressed up gaudy to work in brothels."

"So, he lives off his women. And that's what you call freedom?"

"They don't have to do it; they choose to. He's freer than you or me, or the black gentry who go around aping the white gentry who laugh at their pretensions. I tell you, he's the freest black man in this city!"

"He isn't; he's a slave to his rage. And I don't see what it's gotten him. I respect the quiet ones; no matter what comes, they get on with their lives. My mother was a teacher. Your father was the best black barber in the city and quietly helped his people. Your mother was a healer. They were all among the best. Wasn't that what your father always told you? 'Be the best!' Well, you're one of the best butlers in the city, and everybody knows it. And you don't live in a stinking cellar, or get drunk and bash your friends or the police. I think you've done pretty well, and I admire you for it. In your quiet way you can lord it over some of the richest and most powerful men in this city, and there's nothing they can do about it. As you've often told me, things are not what they seem."

She was quoting Grandpa Jeremiah's words from long ago. I remembered him also saying, "Junius, white folks are strange. It's hard livin' with 'em, but it's even harder livin' without 'em. So, make your peace with that." And again, "Junius, be strong!" So, Thelma's words made sense.

"If I were you," she continued, "I wouldn't go around hurling bricks through windows. You and I have a good thing here. It could be so much worse."

"Well, I suppose so."

"And anyway, who needs all that glittery junk in those stores? We've got more than enough glitter right here."

She had a point. Living at Ida's, I was fulfilling my dream. How many of us do?

After that my anger subsided but didn't die. It was always there: a quiet, bitter resentment. I learned to live with it; I had to. And I got on with my life.

# 20

Ida's second New Year's Day reception was flash indeed, dividing the more sporting of the gentlemen callers with her Fifth Avenue rival, Restell. It was a great success, with a bounty of refreshments and drinks, and frothy conversation. Late that afternoon, as corks popped and vintage clarets flowed, I was called to the door by a solemn-faced man in black, with elegant black kid gloves.

"I'm here for the remains," he announced in a hushed voice.

"What remains?"

"The deceased."

"What deceased?"

"The late departed, of course."

"I think you've got the wrong address."

"Mrs. Clayborn on East Thirty-eighth Street. Please inform her that we're here."

Looking out, I saw a stylish hearse and several attendants at the curb.

When, plucking Ida away from her bubbly guests, I whispered that an undertaker with a hearse was at the door, she winced and her chin dropped an inch. As I followed her out of the parlor, talk was dying down and many eyes were on us.

"Who sent you?" Ida demanded of the caller.

"Madam, I'm not at liberty to say. But I've been instructed to collect the deceased."

"You are instructed to *leave!*" said Ida, and slammed the door.

When we returned to the parlor, china dolls and visitors alike were clustered at the two front windows, watching the shiny black-plumed hearse depart.

"An error or a very bad joke!" Ida announced with an attempt at a smile. To me, with a hiss of venom, she whispered, "Restell!"

After that, the parlor was strangely subdued. Only with the arrival of Mr. Wash did things spark up again.

Thelma and I discussed the incident later.

"Ida thinks it was Restell," I said, "but I doubt it."

"Ida has always called Restell's mansion a palace of death. Some of Ida's guests may have told her. This would be sweet revenge."

"No," I insisted. "Restell inclines to the grandiose. This would be beneath her."

"The Seven Sisters," suggested Thelma. "One or some or all of them."

The Seven Sisters were a row of fancy houses on West Twenty-fifth Street near Seventh Avenue, whose madams were said to be sisters from a small town in New England. The madams ran establishments a notch or two below Ida's, whose outcasts often found shelter there, before resuming their downward spiral. They and Ida were in fierce competition.

"It would be worthy of them," I agreed.

Suddenly Thelma and I were both laughing. To send a hearse to a whorehouse, and on New Year's Day at that! We had witnessed the coup of the season.

Two expulsions marked the spring of '69. Emily, who dressed in virginal white, was found to be squiffy from gin. Thelma and I had long expected it, but couldn't bring ourselves to report it to Ida, as long as there was doubt. Doubt vanished when she showed up tipsy at lunch; Ida banished her on the spot. I helped load her luggage in an express wagon; she was in tears.

"Miss Emily," I said, "if you've had enough of this business, you can go to the Midnight Mission at 206 West Forty-sixth Street. They take in fallen women and help them. They're said to be very welcoming."

She nodded her thanks, saw the express wagon off, and departed on foot, still in tears. I never learned what became of her. Within a day her replacement arrived, Deborah, an ash blonde with a musical voice.

Two weeks later I heard an argument in the library, then a china doll's shout, "Look in the mirror, you wreck!" Summoned by Ida, I found her and Doris of the spit curls in angry confrontation.

"Junius," announced Ida, "Doris is leaving us today. Please see her to her room and off the premises."

I accompanied the girl to her room, an icy silence between us. Suddenly she spun around and faced me.

"Tell the Old Thing I have to make arrangements!"

She went in, slammed the door. Minutes later she reappeared, bonneted, a parasol in hand, and marched downstairs and out the front door with a bang. An hour later she was back, seated in a carriage with a liveried coachman. I helped her load her bandboxes and luggage in the carriage, then wished her luck.

"Tell Wrinklepuss good-bye and good riddance!" she snapped as she got in.

With a command to the coachman, and watched by many eyes peering from windows, she drove off, to what feathered nest we would never know. Linda of the garnet earrings replaced her.

Thelma explained later. Ida's discerning eye had detected in Doris's smooth, young features the barest suggestion of a line or two, a trace of weariness, a hint of the jaded: more than sufficient grounds for expulsion.

"There's a hardness in Ida, isn't there?" I observed.

Thelma shrugged. "It comes with the business. The girls know they won't be here long; two years is the limit. Don't get involved with them; it won't do you or them any good. They're not prisoners; they can leave when they like. Usually they hang on till the end."

After that, Ida summoned me to her room at night more and more often.

"Don't you find, Junius," she asked once, "that it's far more rewarding to remain on the sidelines watching, than to be a part of the comedy?"

"I'm sure it is, ma'am."

"Yes, Junius, I find it immensely satisfying."

So ended the conversation.

Another time I found her seated at her dressing table, studying her features in a hand mirror.

"Sags," she said softly. "A crease."

I of course said nothing. Doris's insults had struck home.

"Do you smell it, Junius?" She gestured toward lace, velvet, gilt.

"What, ma'am?"

"Rotting violets. A taint of mold and semen."

The marble clock on the mantel ticked.

"I smell nothing, ma'am. Nothing at all."

She was scanning herself again in the mirror.

"Is it time for the upstate mansion? Will the taint track me there? I wonder . . ."

She waved me away.

For the first time I realized that my continued sojourn in my beloved brownstone—for sojourn it was—depended on Ida's defenses against sags and creases, and the taint of mold and semen. Her supply of girls could be replenished endlessly, but she herself could not be; she must labor to preserve herself through a sorcery known only to women. On her dressing table were twinkly cut-glass bottles, powder boxes, jars of salves and creams. They reminded me of the clutter on Mrs. Hammond's dressing table, inventoried for me by Rosalie. I had no doubt that Ida would make knowing use of cucumber cream, white wine mixed with rosemary, and God knows what other concoctions, to effect miracles of recuperation. Uneasy, I wished her great success.

I had been courting Thelma all through the winter, hampered by the lack of decent places to take her, oppressed as never before by the color line. I knew of no pleasure garden open to blacks; the dens of the Five Points were out of the question. On the milder days we strolled on quiet side streets, buying snacks from vendors: pineapple candy from a Chinaman; apples from a woman in a tattered calico dress; fruit tarts from a bonneted old lady who kept a stand near Broadway. Ragged boys everywhere offered cheap portraits of Queen Victoria, General Grant, or the latest murderer, and a droll white-haired Englishman sold strops, razors, and knives out of a basket on Nassau Street, while preaching temperance with a wit and humor that kept his audience in stitches. I was grateful to these vendors, who would talk and sell to anyone, and who revealed to Thelma and me yet another aspect of the city.

When spring came, announced to me again in my room by a scent of lilac from the garden below, I got out my gig, polished it, and took Thelma on trips to the Battery and the Park, and even far uptown to the ragged fringe of the city, where shanties and truck gardens encroached on gentlemen's estates before succumbing to the march of paved streets northward. On Harlem Lane we watched in amazement as young bloods aged eighteen to eighty, seated in light wagons, raced their trotters in swirls of dust: yet another pastime of the city's master class, whose strange ways I was still struggling to grasp.

After one of these late-spring outings, having dropped Thelma off a block from the brownstone and returned the gig to the livery stable, I came back to find her waiting for me in the hall. Our eyes met; she let me take her hand. Going in silence up the back stairs to my room, we entered and shut the door. It was early evening; I lit candles and opened the window curtains to let in a flow of milky moonlight scented with mock orange from the garden. I started to speak, but she put a finger on my lips to hush me. In silence I removed Dilly's quilt from the bed, pulled back the covers. Wordlessly we undressed, reclined on the bed, embraced, kissed. As I had hoped, she gave herself interestingly, and with mystery; at the first thrust in, I spent. Again she put her finger to my lips, smiled. We did it a second and then a third time, and this last time we spent together. We fell asleep in each other's arms; at dawn she dressed and tiptoed out. It had been dreamlike yet amazingly simple. From that day on, I thought of her as my wife.

❦

Summer came, bringing a fragrance of honeysuckle into my room. By day Thelma and I worked side by side as always; by night she came to me, put her finger on my lips, and gave herself. By late summer the peach tree in the garden was laden with fruit. Dennis harvested all he could reach and piled them in a bowl in the kitchen, to enrich the meals of the girls and the help. I bit into the peaches greedily, shredding the warm, soft flesh till my teeth scraped the pit, and my chin dripped with juices, and my fingers were wet and sticky. Watching me, Thelma smiled in complicity.

At the top of the tree, well out of Dennis's reach, were the plumpest sun-ripened peaches, which finally plopped on the ground and split open, a feast for bees and wasps. From my room I couldn't hear them plop, but the aroma of full, ripe peaches rose to me, excited me. Sleeping with Thelma, I felt that all the ripeness of the earth had been given into my hands at last.

❧

"Junius, I have some matters to discuss with you."

Ida had summoned me to the library, where she was looking over accounts at her desk. The voice she used was not the dreamy one tinged with bitterness of her late-night musings, but the brisk daytime voice of the woman of authority.

"As you know, I consider you and Thelma my eyes and ears in this establishment."

"Yes ma'am, and we're honored by your trust."

"But I also have eyes and ears of my own. So, I know that you and Thelma have not always been forthcoming."

"How do you mean, Miz Ida?"

"You tell me what it suits you to tell me, but keep the rest to yourselves."

By now I was sweating. There was plenty we hadn't told her about others—we didn't like snitching—or for that matter, about ourselves.

"Regarding the help, Miz Ida, there's nothing to report. They're all fiercely loyal to you and do their jobs well."

"I was not thinking of the help—of the others, at least."

"As for the young ladies, I confess that we've overlooked a few peccadilloes, but nothing that would compromise you or your establishment."

"Junius, it is for me, not you, to decide what is or is not a peccadillo. Is that understood?"

"Yes ma'am."

"You and Thelma are not without some peccadilloes of your own. Taking all those items from the storeroom, for instance, without my permission."

"Miz Ida, not one of them has ever left this brownstone, or ever will."

"See that they don't. There are other matters that I could also mention, but for the moment will not. Do not abuse my patience. You'll be in charge here during my vacation. I expect everything to proceed as if I were here myself."

"Yes ma'am."

"You and Thelma have served me well. I wouldn't like having to dismiss you."

"You wouldn't do that, Miz Ida."

"Do not put me to the test. That's all for now, Junius. We'll talk again after my return."

This was the first time she had ever mentioned the possibility of dismissing me. Of course I reported the whole conversation to Thelma, who pondered.

"Hmm . . . She knows something but doesn't say what. Clever. This way she's got us nervous, yet she may not know much at all."

"What's this about a vacation?"

"Since August is our slow month, she's decided to go upstate for a breath of fresh mountain air. Of course I'll have to go with her."

This hurt. "For how long?"

"Two weeks, maybe three. I don't like it either, but it can't be helped. You'll be in charge here, quite a responsibility. She's never done this before; it shows she trusts you. But be careful while she's away. Above all, watch out for Linda."

Linda of the garnet earrings, the latest arrival, was a small, pert redhead much in demand among the gentlemen callers, yet all that summer she had singled me out.

"Good morning, handsome Junius," she would greet me every morning in the hallway, though I had paid her scant attention.

"Junius," she said once in a cajoling, almost whining voice, "don't frown at little me. Smile!" So, I felt obliged to smile.

Often one or another of her admirers would call for her in a carriage and take her on an afternoon outing. As she sortied in a handsome day dress, her reddish hair topped by a pillbox hat, she would whisper to me in the vestibule, "Handsome Junius, these men are frightful bores!" This without the slightest encouragement from me.

Or in the hallway, when no one else was about, she might wink, blow a kiss, or stick her tongue out in passing, gestures that I studiously ignored.

"Be careful," Thelma had warned me, when I first informed her of these seeming advances. "A born troublemaker. She flirts, gossips, teases, sulks, but never enough for Ida to censure her. The men like her and it's gone to her head. The other girls either adore her or absolutely loathe her. Keep away!"

Easier said than done. "Handsome Junius, I reserve you," was her next hallway greeting, followed by a spate of declarations spiced with a hint of derision. I didn't know how seriously to take them:

"Junius, have you no heart?"

"Junius, you shall not escape!"

"Junius, you make me weep diamonds of tears!"

All these comments I had received with the most noncommittal "hello" or "good day," then distanced myself at once. Having my brownstone and Thelma, I wasn't going to be compromised by this silly little flirt. Finally she assumed a pouting expression tinged at times with a trace of malice.

"Junius, you skate on thin ice."

"Junius, you're playing with fire."

"Junius, I can read you like a book. I *know*, Junius, I *know!*"

What indeed did the little bitch know? Thelma and I had been the most discreet of lovers and had never caught her snooping. But now she had planted a suspicion; it grew and festered.

Soon after that, Ida and Thelma departed. Dennis and I loaded their luggage onto an express wagon bound for the docks, then saw them into Ida's carriage, bound for the same. A steamboat would take them to a resort in the Hudson Highlands perched high above the river on a bluff. Waves, cheery good-byes. Facing our first separation, Thelma and I bore up remarkably well. As Dennis and I went back up the stoop, Linda met us at the top.

"So, the Old Thing's gone at last! Thank heavens! Now the fun can begin."

Saying this, she shot me a quick hot glance. It unnerved me.

# 21

IN IDA'S ABSENCE I WAS IN COMPLETE CHARGE OF THE brownstone; at the very thought of it, a thrill shot through me. I oversaw the daily operations as usual, made sure the girls received their callers (few in number) properly, and totaled each day's receipts. Then, every other day, following Ida's specific instructions, I sortied in her carriage to deposit her own and the china dolls' earnings, stashed in Ida's Russian leather pouch, in the steel vaults of the Bank of New York. Departing, I made a point of going down the steep front stoop, shunning the basement entrance reserved for deliverymen and the help. Getting into the carriage in my best frock coat and topper, I always winked at John the coachman, who smiled slyly but otherwise treated me like his master. When the carriage stopped in front of the bank on Wall Street, and I, a black man, got out and went inside to make my deposits, I got plenty of stares. I played it straight-faced, while laughing to myself.

With Ida gone, I often slipped into her bedroom to gaze again at the four-poster with its carved mahogany posts, and caress the silk damask hangings and the counterpane of blue brocade. Having fantasized endlessly about the bed, I longed to actually sleep in it and was strongly tempted to, but one thing held me back: a little bitch named Linda.

The moment Ida was gone, Linda had resumed her hallway tauntings and flirtations mixed with threats, which I made a point of ignoring. Then she began greeting me daily with a jingle:

Handsome Junius, cold and callous,
Rules the roost in Ida's palace,
Sneaks and spies and lurks and snitches.
O to singe his bawdy britches!

At first she recited it singsong, then she sang it, ending with a giggle. I played deaf, but heard it so often that the words were stamped on my brain. Finally I addressed her:

"Miss Linda, you surely know that Madam Ida has left me fully in charge here. I can ask you to leave at any time. Don't think I wouldn't do it."

She smirked. "Handsome Junius, you wouldn't dare! I know too much about you."

"You know nothing. Push me enough and I will."

I was bluffing, in the hopes that she too was bluffing: risky. When the taunts and jingle continued, I surprised her with some verses of my own:

Taunting Linda, deft with verses,
Flirts and giggles, sulks and curses,
Expelled from Ida's, fall complete,
Flaunts her titties on the street.

Not great poetry, but she got the message. Soon after that she switched her attentions to Philip the waiter, rendering the poor fellow so nervous that his hands shook when serving drinks to guests in the parlor.

❧

Shortly before she left with Ida, Thelma had discovered Dilly's Bible quilt in my room and marveled at it. Learning that I had two aunts living in the city, she asked if she could meet them. They took to her at once, and she to them. When she praised Dilly's Freedom quilt, Dilly got teary-eyed and announced, "Honey, you make me too happy to see straight!" As for Bessie, she and Thelma, an ex-teacher, ended up swapping stories that could be told to schoolchildren, and Bessie thanked her repeatedly for some new ideas. Now, when I paid them a visit, the subject of Thelma came up at once.

"She's a peach," said Dilly. "She's just one in a million!"

"You marry her," said Bessie, "and don't shilly-shally, or some other blood beat your time. Oh Junius, I'm just starved for a weddin'!"

I tried to explain that, for many reasons, there would be no wedding soon. How could there be, given Ida's opposition to relationships among her help? Of course they thought Thelma and I worked in a respectable brownstone.

"Junius," said Dilly, "we gonna pray to the Lord. Bessie and I don't pray for the same thing often; we too fractious. But when we do, the Lord's just got to listen!"

❧

Back at the brownstone, the situation with Linda was coming to a head. She flirted with the help, made mocking comments to me, came and went as she pleased. One morning she announced:

"Handsome Junius, Mr. Wash has invited me to Long Branch for a week. I leave this afternoon."

This was interesting, since I knew for a fact that Mr. Wash had stashed his family for a month at Saratoga, where he would presumably join them soon.

"Miss Linda, you know the rules. You can't leave here for any length of time without Madam Ida's prior consent."

"Oh pooh! She's off upstate somewhere. *You* can give me permission."

"No, I can't, Miss Linda. I don't have the authority."

"Then I'll go without permission. So there!" She stuck her tongue out at me like a schoolgirl.

"If you do, Miss Linda, I'll have to inform Madam Ida. You may not be allowed to return."

"Ida would let me go, if she were here, and she'll let me come back in a week. Mr. Wash will pay her generously."

"It won't work, Miss Linda."

"Junius, those silly rules don't apply to *me. I* have connections!"

And she flounced off with a giggle.

Of course she meant Mr. Wash, who called for her in a carriage after lunch. Off she went, all frills and flounces, under a parasol of bright pink silk.

I wired Ida the news, expecting an order for her immediate expulsion. But Ida's response surprised me: DO NOTHING UNTIL I RETURN. Ida had always shown Mr. Wash an unusual indulgence, but now she was tolerating—at least for the moment—a flagrant flouting of her rules. Did Mr. Wash have something on Ida? I was baffled.

❧

With Ida and Linda both out of the brownstone, I could realize my fantasy at last. Night after night, unobserved, I tiptoed into Ida's bedroom, locked the door, and approached the towering mahogany four-poster. Parting the rose-colored silk damask hangings, I turned back the counterpane of blue brocade, slipped naked between silken sheets, and reclined on the softest of down mattresses amid aromas of polished mahogany, lavender, and mint. I imagined Thelma/Sheba/Cleopatra joining me in that silken paradise; raptures resulted. Of course I took great care not to leave any trace on the bed.

I took full advantage as well of the wash basin with gleaming silver-plated faucets, the dolphin-shaped commode, and finally, for a further taste of Elysium, the monumental marble-encased tub, where I bathed voluptuously, using Ida's scented soaps. What more to yearn for? To have Thelma herself—the real Thelma, not some seductive illusion—with me in that bed, and in the tub as well. Then, and only then, perhaps, would my possession of the brownstone be complete. Impossible, so it seemed, but what is life but yearning? So, I yearned.

❧

One week to the day after her departure, Linda returned from Long Branch, talking blithely of costume balls and hops, fashions, and the afternoon parade of carriages; the other girls listened in envy and awe. Then, two days later, Ida and Thelma arrived, at which point Linda subsided a little, without ceasing to be a center of attention. Thelma and I had not exchanged letters, lest we arouse Ida's suspicions, but Ida's attitude toward me was pinched with a chill. Something had changed.

In the library I handed her the keys and the Russian leather pouch she carried cash in to the bank, and submitted the accounts. She glanced at them, approved.

"Junius, you are of course wondering why I am so tolerant of Linda's obvious lapses, and for that matter of Mr. Wash's untoward behavior since the start in puffing his railroad in the parlor."

"Yes, Miz Ida, I am."

"It's very simple: Mr. Wash has connections."

That word again. Mr. Wash, Linda, Ida herself—everyone, apparently, but me—seemed to have connections.

"Oh."

"For this reason, and this reason alone, I am inclined to overlook certain improprieties. In time this will all be attended to. However"—she shot me a look—"there are other matters I shall not overlook."

I waited, said nothing, sweated.

"I mean, of course, you and Thelma. I am not the fool you take me for. A satisfied woman radiates joy, and those who have known such joy can detect it. Long ago—very briefly—I knew such joy, and I see it now in Thelma. You and she have been thick as thieves long since. This clandestine affair, this little amour of yours, must stop."

So, here it was at last: the confrontation. Since Ida needed to have control in every aspect of her life, she saw my desire to be with Thelma as a challenge. But I loved Thelma, couldn't live without her, and wouldn't let Ida's disillusion with love ruin my future.

"Miz Ida, it can't stop. Thelma and I are in love; we want to get married."

"It *must* stop. I will not have my house corrupted with dirty little secret trysts and affairs."

"I see. You only permit the copulation of whores and their customers, since that brings in money."

Her green eyes flashed. "I will take no insolence from a servant! If you won't break off this so-called amour, you can pack your bags and leave!"

"Miz Ida, I cannot and will not break it off."

She stood up in towering majesty and pointed to the door. *"Go!"*

I didn't budge.

"Did you hear me, Junius? I'm dismissing you here and now. Go!"

"Miz Ida, you can't dismiss me. You need me and Thelma more than we need you."

She clenched both fists. "I need no one! Servants are easily replaced."

"Not me, and not Thelma either. She's the best personal maid you ever had, and I'm the best butler. You can replace us, but it wouldn't be the same. I've always admired you as a shrewd businesswoman, and as such you can't act against your own interest. Thelma and I are a part of this brownstone; we belong here and help make it function. It's ours as well as yours."

Dumbfounded, she sat back down in her chair. "No servant has ever talked to me like this!"

"Think of us as your partners. If Thelma and I are involved in what you call an amour, that binds us to each other and to you. You should welcome discreet romances among the help. If they're happy, they'll stay longer. The last thing you need here is constant changes in staff. Revise your rules a bit; things will go more smoothly."

"So, now you're telling me how to run my business!"

"*Our* business. We're all in this together."

Silence; she gave me a hard look. I met her gaze.

"Miz Ida, you're strong and I'm strong; we're a match."

For a moment she showed the faintest hint of a smile. But then her eyes narrowed to hot green slits. "Junius, I shall take under advisement all that you have said. But be warned: I'm a hard woman. You shan't get round me easily. You have been presumptuous; I shall not forget."

"Miz Ida, I ask only that you act in your own self-interest, nothing more."

"You will hear from me shortly. Go!"

As I left the library, I felt her fierce gaze following me out.

❧

"You told her she couldn't fire us?" Thelma was stunned. As usual, we were conferring in the linen closet.

"Not if she's the smart businesswoman I think she is."

"Ida has to have control, and you challenged her! We might as well both start packing."

"I'm not so sure."

"I am! In all the time I've been with her, she's never backed down once."

If Thelma was stunned by this news, she was twice as stunned when I told her how I'd slept in Ida's bed.

"You're crazy—absolutely crazy!"

"I'd dreamed of it for months. It was prime."

"You go too far!"

"No obsession can ever go too far!"

When I delivered this ringing pronouncement, on Thelma's face I saw bafflement and a flicker of fear, warning of conflict to come. Then Dennis arrived, visibly shaken.

"Junius, Miz Ida gave me a message for you. You're to be off the premises by five."

"You see?" said Thelma. "Now we'll both have to go."

I had gambled and lost; so be it. "All right, I'd better start packing."

"So will I," said Thelma.

"No, wait."

"Why?"

"I don't know. Just wait."

Leaving Thelma to explain to Dennis and the others, I went to my room and started packing. Everything that Ida had given me or loaned me I would leave; everything that I owned I would take. I was riled.

Consternation erupted in the brownstone. As the news spread, one by one the staff came to confirm it, register shock and dismay, and bid me a reluctant good-bye. Julie was in tears; John and Philip shook their heads in disbelief; Marie the cook, usually quiet and docile, muttered, "That woman don't know what she's doin'!" Even the china dolls, though they kept a distance, were troubled: if it could happen to me, it could happen to anyone.

When I had two bags full, I took them down to the vestibule. Bessie and Dilly always had my old room in the garret ready for me. I would leave my bags there and come back for the rest of my belongings. Yes, Old Thing, I would be out by five!

Out of my brownstone, where I had lived so long and so richly! Only now did I grasp what I would have to give up: the polished wood surfaces, the velvets and silks and brocades, the knickknacks and gewgaws that I had touched and breathed and loved. Thelma I could take with me, but not these; it would hurt.

Dennis caught me at the top of the stoop: "She wants to see you in the library."

Putting my bags down, I went. Still sitting at her desk, she didn't look up when I entered.

"Junius, you will resume your duties. And because you and Thelma have served me exceptionally well, I'm doubling your wages. Please keep this to yourselves; I cannot be so generous with everyone. That is all. You may go."

Not once had she looked me in the eye.

Yet again, the news spread quickly through the brownstone, inspiring a universal sigh of relief.

When everyone had finished welcoming me back, Thelma pulled me into the linen closet.

"Why would she do that? Let you go and then bring you back?"

"She's a hard-headed businesswoman. She knows that what I said is true: she needs you and me to help run the brownstone. But she can't lose face in front of everyone. She had to let me go to show that she had the power, but then keep me on so we can help run this place. I know this and so does Ida, but we won't tell the others."

A new respect now greeted me as the only one who had ever stood up to Ida and come out on top. I think she may even have admired me for it. But I didn't strut; it had been too close a thing. Luck like this couldn't happen twice.

# 22

THE COMPLETION OF THE FIRST TRANSCONTINENTAL railroad spurred Mr. Wash on to greater heights of rhetoric in promoting his own westward enterprise. But during his frequent visits to the brownstone, where he continued to lavish attention on Linda, he at times addressed a few words to me.

"Junius, before I made my money, I was known as 'that fast-talkin' bastard from Peoria.' Now I'm 'Mr. Burns.'"

I smiled.

"Junius, do you know this city?"

"As much as a black man can, Mr. Wash. I was born here. I've seen Broadway and its side streets, the Battery, the markets, the docks, the Central Park, and Harlem Lane."

"Then you've seen more than I have. Quite a place, ain't it? Since I come here, I been flattered, taunted, sneered at, put down, fleeced, and riled, but I never been bored."

"Neither have I, Mr. Wash."

"I come here from Peoria by way of St. Louis and Chicago. Chicago's a great little town, just leaped up out of nowhere, and I love it. But New York's special, ain't it? It's just the goin'est place."

"I know what you mean, Mr. Wash."

"Junius, don't ever leave this city, unless you're tired of life."

Just then some friends plucked him away for a drink, and soon afterward, Linda being occupied, he was presented to Deborah of the musical voice, who eyed him with interest over the flutterings of a tortoiseshell fan.

I marveled: this master of puffery, this artist of razzle-dazzle, was almost becoming a friend! Yet I could not get free of my first impression that in some vague, indefinable way, he was a threat to me and my brownstone.

❧

That fall I seemed to be a magnet for confidences. Ida often summoned me to her room at night, as if nothing untoward had ever passed between us. Usually she was sitting in the rocking chair, a glass of sherry at hand. She spoke several times of her second lover, who had often clasped her throat in a menacing way.

"He slipped so often and so easily from the embrace of love to the embrace of death, that I could hardly tell them apart. Droll, don't you think?"

I knew to make no answer. Then, another time:

"Junius, the clasp of love is the clasp of death. There is no difference."

Were these comments a sour old woman's effort to squelch a love shared by others that she had never known?

"Junius," she said yet another time, "for every woman death is a man, a glittering seducer. And for every man death is a woman, sensual and cunning. Whether she is called Madonna or Venus or Eve or the Whore of Babylon makes no difference. She is a cock-trap; you will not escape her."

That said, she waved me away.

I had once admired this woman. At times now, I swung between pity and hate.

❧

One Monday when Thelma couldn't get away, I went driving by myself in the Park. As another gig passed me going in the same direction, the driver called my name and waved: Lester, accompanied by a young woman in a beribboned bonnet that looked vaguely familiar. When we pulled off the Drive and stopped, I met the usual expansive greeting. He was wearing his natty felt bowler and his trousers with braiding down the side, and his gig looked new and shiny.

"Why, Junius Fox, of all people!" cried his bonneted companion: Rosalie Wood, whom I hadn't seen since leaving Mrs. Hammond's. She was wearing the lavender dress with a black belt and gold buckle that I remembered well from her mysterious outings, and held a pink parasol to fend off the sun. We explained our connection to Lester.

"Aren't you smart!" she exclaimed, looking me up and down. "Oh Junius, aren't you flash! You've come a long ways since Mrs. Hammond's, but then"—she giggled—"haven't we all?"

I agreed that we had.

"Lester's been showing me the Park in his fancy thingamabob—"

"Gig," said Lester.

"—and we've had a smashing good time! All kinds of barouches and whatchamacallits on the Drive, and sporting blades with their girls, and old ladies primped up quaint. White folks sure do cut a shine, but then"—another giggle—"so do we!"

This was the old Rosalie, lively, flippant, coy: the tease. While Lester beamed, she rattled on just a bit nervously. Maybe she was worried about my knowing of her abortion, but her secret was safe with me. Lester and I agreed to meet that evening in a black-owned bar off Broadway where we had met before; a bit dingy, but where else could we talk?

"Good-bye, you flash young blade!" said Rosalie, as she and Lester drove off.

Over an ale that evening Lester and I exchanged intelligence about Mr. Wash. I reported his doings at Madam Ida's, while Lester catalogued his family—a social-climbing wife and four children—and described in awe his employer's meteoric rise from modest beginnings as a hardware dealer in Peoria to the vice presidency of a railroad. Flash times!

"Where *is* Peoria?" I asked.

"In Kansas, I think."

"And if he's the V.P., who's the president?"

"Hmm, I don't know. He never mentions it."

"Are you sure this railroad is on the up and up?"

"Absolutely. He's given me some shares. I've seen documents on his desk. They'll be laying track next spring."

"He's a great talker."

"And a great doer."

We agreed that to the depths of his diamonded shirtfront, and the bright, hard twinkle of his studs, Mr. Wash was flash.

As for Rosalie, "She's my hot toddy," Lester announced. "My artichoke, my sine qua non."

Soon after that I saw Mr. Wash at Ida's sitting alone in the library, where, since Philip was busy elsewhere, I served him a whiskey cobbler.

"Junius, you're a nobody and I'm a nobody, yet here we are in the fanciest whorehouse in the city, rubbin' elbows with bluebloods and muckamucks. Funny, ain't it?"

"You could say that, Mr. Wash."

"Junius, I'm nobody out of nowhere. Know what I was before the war? A hardware dealer in Peoria, sellin' nuts and bolts. That's all I was: nuts and bolts."

I stood at hand, said nothing.

"Then the war came and I heard the Army in St. Louis was hard up for tents, uniforms, guns—you name it. So, I went there, made some contacts, and pulled off some deals. Money was just sloshin' around, and I sluiced some into my pocket. Then I and the little woman went to Chicago to get rid of some of that jack. We had a blast. But then I heard about New York: more government contracts, gobs of money, a real flash place to be. 'Wash,' says the missus, 'let's go there!' So, here we are. Know what she's doin' now? Learnin' French. Learnin' etiquette. And givin' fancy parties. She's a comer, all right, more push than poise. Like me: Wash Burns from Peoria, V.P., P.P.R. A nobody turned somebody. Like you, Junius, like you."

He eyed me over his half-filled tumbler, his features drawn, his eye bright. His hand trembled slightly.

"'Cause you're up from nowhere, too. A black man in a white man's world, but you're goin' somewhere. You may not know quite where, but you're goin'. Junius, we gotta dream, we gotta dare. That's what this country's all about: dream, dare, do: America! So, here's to you, Junius. Good luck!"

He raised his glass to me and drank: the only one of Ida's guests who ever did. I was surprised and just a bit moved.

"Thank you, Mr. Wash."

After that, he gazed off into space.

A week later I saw him alone in the library again. This time he didn't even glance at me, just stared straight ahead.

"Junius, in this life you go and go and go. There just ain't nothin' else."

He looked tired.

Who was this man and what was he after? Was he a visionary or a madman, a fool or a fraud? What did his vision mean for me, a black man? Could I share in it? At times I wanted to, but the memory of a certain incident in a jewelry shop on Broadway sobered me. And if his railroad—assuming it existed—got to the Pacific, would he be satisfied with that? Wouldn't he yearn for the Orient, the world? I had yearned for a brownstone and got it; what more did I need? But was that brownstone mine, really mine? Or was I a dreamer, too? We all have our illusions. Mr. Wash made me look for mine. I was nervous.

❧

By now I had seen Restell in the Park several times. Once, while strolling there, I saw her walking toward me, elegant as always, under a fringed green silk parasol. The other promenaders were eyeing her, but no one greeted her. As she approached, I tipped my hat and bowed. Puzzled, she gave a slight civil nod and, with a hint of a smile, walked on. I too was smiling—at her poise, my boldness, and the social comedy being played out. Regarding abortion I had mixed feelings at best, but I admired the woman's need of risk, her daring: a worthy rival for Ida.

When December came, anticipation of the New Year's Day receptions became intense among the city's sporting element. Of course it was assumed that Ida and Restell would contend furiously to attract gentlemen callers. Ida sent out quantities of silk-fringed invitations engraved with an elegant script. The parlors were rigorously cleaned, the tea and coffee urns polished, crystal made to shine, and antique serving spoons of solid silver put out beside wine decanters and a display of fruit, cakes, pies, and puddings. Fires crackled on the hearths, and bits of glass hanging in the windows cast rainbowed flecks of light over the well-busted Venuses of bronze. Conspicuously displayed on the wall was a newly acquired *Apotheosis of Cupid* in oils, showing a well-endowed nude youth rising triumphant in the sky over a troop of adoring nymphs and chubby infants, not one of them hampered by clothing; it was said to have cost thousands.

I myself got so caught up in the spirit of the moment that I gave an extra shine to my shoes and rubbed each button and stud till it glittered. The china dolls came down wearing low-cut, ruffled dresses, and Ida herself appeared in a green overskirt over a crimson dress fringed with black lace, her masses of dark hair topped by a silver tiara. No question, the Old Thing had pulled it off again.

Word of these preparations brought the gentlemen out in droves through weather that alternated moments of sunlight with a quiet sifting of snow. From one o'clock on I was kept busy receiving the callers' cards and announcing them to Ida in the parlor, where the scent of their locks slick with Macassar oil mingled with the ladies' perfumes. Once again Dennis was hanging the visitors' coats and hats in the hallway, Thelma and Julie were bringing more refreshments as needed, and Philip was serving delicacies to guests from a tray. Meanwhile I was depositing the cards in the silver card receiver on a stand in the hall. As instructed by Ida, I was keeping a rough count of their number, which at intervals I whispered to Thelma, who whispered it in turn to Ida. Ida, having received seventy-three cards the previous year, was hoping now to snag at least eighty-five.

By late afternoon, with some seventy cards lodged in the receiver, the hostess had high hopes. Besides the regulars, Ida's parlor was packed with bankers, lawyers, merchants, railroad men, aldermen, and blades about town. Conversation ran to fine wines, turnouts, horses, country estates, and plans for European travel, with an occasional risqué anecdote told well out of the hostess's hearing. Once again I noted bloods, senescents, and satyrs, though toward the satyrs I nursed a newfound tolerance prompted by bitter memories of my bout with Liza Ann. At six o'clock I whispered to Thelma the impressive count of seventy-eight.

Soon after, Mr. Wash arrived.

"Didn't give up on me, now did you, Junius? I've saved the best till last!"

He handed me a card that glittered, surrendered his coat and hat to Dennis, and breezed into the parlor before I could announce him. There he kissed Ida on both cheeks, winked and waved at the girls. Then, after the usual spiel puffing his railroad, he summoned ice-filled buckets of champagne.

"Here's to 1870," he announced. "Champagne for all—my treat!"

Corks popped, champagne flowed; bubbly glasses were raised by all. Watching as usual from the doorway, I marveled; once again, in a scant few minutes he had taken over, was now proposing toast after toast.

"To Madam Ida and her troop of belles, the most outrageously lovely ladies in the city!"

Glasses clinked; cries of "Hear! Hear!" Beaming, the ladies hid behind their fans or cast their eyes demurely on the floor.

"To this great Go Ahead city, the locomotive of these United States, pullin' the rest of the country into the eye-poppin' world of tomorrow!"

More clinks, more cries of "Hear! Hear!"

"To railroads—they conquer the wilderness, bind whole continents, bring civilization and wealth to all!"

"To railroads!" chorused the crowd, taking another sip with each toast. The whole room was now completely under his spell.

"To this rumbustious nation, under God, its destiny—"

He paused; we waited, anticipating some grandiose vision of the future. His mouth moved but not a word came out. He tensed, gasped, wavered—was the man drunk?—then toppled headlong, knocking a tray of goblets from Philip's hands as he fell, sprawling face down amid debris of shattered glass.

Stunned, the crowd drew back; a few smiled indulgently; Ida dropped her fan. Rushing into the room, I kneeled, turned him over. Purple-faced, mouth agape, he stared. This was no drunk. I closed his eyes. "He's dead."

# 23

My words provoked an exodus. The gentlemen fled pell-mell, grabbing their coats and hats from a startled Dennis and stampeding out the front door and down the stoop. A police investigation was sure to follow; they wanted no part of it.

"Junius," said Ida, "get the girls to their rooms."

They needed little persuasion, fleeing readily from the purple-faced corpse on the floor. Once I had seen them all into their rooms, I returned to the parlor, where Thelma and Julie were sweeping up the glass on the carpet. When my eyes met Thelma's, we exchanged a look of shock and astonishment.

"Dennis," said Ida, "you will seek Dr. Rhodes at this address. Junius, you will deliver this note to Mr. Blake at the address indicated. If he's not at home, wait. Tell him that it's urgent."

We left, Dennis hurrying to an address nearby, and I to one on East Sixteenth Street over toward the river. It was dark, with hints of snow. Lighted windows and hurrying carriages showed that calls were still being made. The address proved to be a row house with no service entrance; I knocked at the front door. An Irish maid answered, scowling.

"What business be so urgent, that you must bother us when we're cleanin' up after a slew o' callers?"

"Miss, it's urgent."

I gave her the note, waited while she took it inside. Minutes later Mr. Blake appeared, a heavyset man with a handlebar mustache. I recognized him as the detective who had accompanied the minister in Ida's parlor.

"Tell her I'll be there as soon as I can."

I nodded, left.

Back at Ida's the splintered glass had all been swept up, and the servants were removing dishes and decanters from the parlor. The doctor was examining the body, with Ida and Dennis in close attendance.

"Stroke," he said as I came in.

Having heard my report, Ida paced up and down on the carpet, somewhat agitated, until the knocker announced Mr. Blake. He took a close look at the body, then conferred with Ida and the doctor in whispers. Dennis and I waited at a distance. Several times we heard Ida speak with fierce insistence:

"The body must be removed at once!"

The whispered conference continued; some resolution was finally achieved.

"Dennis and Junius," Ida announced, her voice quivering slightly, "Mr. Wash has had one too many. Please see him safely home. Mr. Blake will get a cab."

So, the corpse would be delivered home as if drunk! Better for both the family and Ida. I traded a look of wonder with Dennis.

While the detective was fetching a cab—not easy on the evening of New Year's Day—Dennis, Philip, and I with great effort managed to get Mr. Wash's overcoat on him, pulled his topper down tight on his head, and carried him down the front hallway stairs to the basement entrance, so as to avoid a display on the stoop. Mr. Wash wasn't light, but at least the body as yet wasn't stiff. When Mr. Blake arrived with a cab, we carried Mr. Wash out, his feet dragging, and with the detective's help got him up into it. From his high seat the driver watched curiously, said nothing. Blake, Dennis, and I got inside with the corpse. Blake gave the driver an address on the upper Fifth Avenue, and off we went. En route not a word was spoken.

We arrived in front of a fancy brownstone, where the front parlor lights were still lit: the aftermath of another reception. As we dragged Mr. Wash from the cab, a light snow was falling; it tickled my nose and chin. Blake told the cab to wait, then helped us maneuver the body around to the service entrance under the stoop, where Blake yanked the bellpull. After a long wait, an aproned maid opened the door. Blake mumbled something and flashed his badge, then we carried the body into the vestibule and gently let it slump down at the feet of the astonished girl. Blake tipped his hat, we left, got into the cab, and trotted off. Fifteen minutes later Blake deposited Dennis and myself at the curb in front of Ida's and hurried off in the cab. The whole thing seemed unreal.

Back in the parlor everything had been set right; no trace of the death remained.

"Ida's gone up to her room," Thelma reported. "She looked terrible."

On the stand in the hall the silver bowl was heaped to the brim with cards that had yet to be counted. On top was Mr. Wash's, the flashiest of them all, bearing a charming winter scene with ground glass imitating snow. On an impulse I put it in my pocket. Minutes later I went upstairs and stumbled into bed. I didn't get much sleep.

❧

At breakfast in the kitchen the next morning, the servants talked about Mr. Wash and little else.

"What happened to the body?" asked Marie.

"It's been seen to," said Dennis.

"How?" asked Philip.

"Never mind," I said. "It's been seen to. That's enough."

Later Thelma caught me in the hall alone. "She's locked herself in her room, won't answer when I knock."

"I wouldn't worry. Like all of us, she's shook up. She needs to be alone."

I saw to it that the parlor floor was cleaned and straightened as always, and fresh flowers installed in the vases. Then I counted the cards in the receiver: with Mr. Wash's, eighty-eight. Toward noon the girls began drifting down for lunch. From the kitchen I could hear them in the dining room.

"Wasn't that something?"

"Gave me the willies."

"Me, too. I couldn't sleep. Kept seeing that face of his splotched purple."

"I'm not hungry."

"Where's Ida?"

"That's what I'd like to know."

"Still in her room, I think."

"Why? What's the Old Thing up to?"

"Shh . . . !"

"Up to? Who knows?"

Not a word about *Godey's Lady's Book* or the *Journal des Demoiselles.* Later I checked with Thelma in the linen closet.

"She still won't let me in. I'm worried."

"Is she sick?"

"I don't think so. I hear her moving around. But she won't say a word when I knock."

"She's upset. She'll come round in time."

"This has never happened before."

"Before this, no one ever died in her parlor."

"Why don't *you* try tonight? Maybe she'll open to you."

That afternoon some of the girls waited in the parlor, though no gentleman had made an appointment. They sat or moved languidly about, talked little. Silent in their cages, even the canaries seemed to mope. That evening two or three gentlemen appeared, but the conversation languished, and the girl at the pianoforte played listlessly; not one caller went upstairs. The girls shrugged, went to bed early.

Later, I knocked softly on Ida's door.

"Miz Ida, it's Junius."

No answer. I knocked again; no answer. Thelma appeared in the hall; I shook my head, shrugged. We went to our separate rooms; no thought of love crossed our minds. In my room I retrieved Mr. Wash's card from my pocket, put it on my dresser; it glittered.

What was going on in Ida's room? I remembered how Big Sue, when down, got drunk and spoke her heart out in plain sight of her customers and girls, without a trace of embarrassment or shame. For Ida, such public loss of control was inconceivable.

❧

The next day was no different; our knocks brought no response. I imagined her on the bed or in the rocking chair, staring at a white ceiling drubbed by the ticking of the marble clock. Was it time at last for the upstate mansion?

The upstate mansion . . . I imagined the maple-shaded avenue, the smooth lawn, the wide front porch. Bay windows and balconies and turrets, potted shrubs, vines on trellises, and eaves with gingerbread molding. Large rooms with ottomans and huge hearths. Clean, well lit. Genteel conversation from the lady callers, as Ida, clothed smartly in black silk laced with gold, pours tea from a silver pot. Ida the regal, the respectable. Whom the mayor calls on, hat in hand. Signing checks for charities. Giving money to a local college, its halls stuffed with classics and the Bible and well-scrubbed, pink-faced students. Reading her philosophers under the bare white ceiling, while sipping bitter coffee and smiling her scant, pinched smile. Till the taint reaches her, the smell of mold and semen . . .

Would it happen? Would Thelma and I go with her? Could I give up the excitement of the city, and my beloved brownstone, for this fragile refuge from decay? How I hated Wash Burns for his death!

❧

Later in the morning Dennis brought me a newspaper: "Mr. G. Washington Burns, patriot, financier, vice president of the Peoria & Pacific Railroad. Died quietly at home."

So, we had brought it off. Lester and I would have to exchange reports.

❧

That evening not one caller came; word had got round. But when I knocked on Ida's door, she answered.

"Come in, Junius."

The door was unlocked; I entered. She was sitting in a silk robe at her dressing table, her hair down loose about her shoulders, studying herself in her mirror. She spoke softly.

"Did you know, Junius, that lace rots, that marble melts?"

"No ma'am."

"They do."

"Miz Ida, you're missed downstairs."

"There is death in the parlor, Junius. Walls drip, vases stink."

"We've cleaned it up. And scrubbed the vases and changed the flowers just like always."

She looked up at me, old, tired, worn, her face wrinkled like finely cracked plaster. I was shocked.

"You may go, Junius. In the morning you can bring me a broth."

I left. Behind me I heard the click of the latch.

Later, Thelma came to my room for a report.

"She says there's death in the parlor, and looks like death herself. She's older—much older than I realized."

"Of course," said Thelma.

"And sick. We've got to heal her."

"I'm not a healer, and you aren't either."

"You healed me that time I had the fever."

"You healed yourself. I and the others helped."

"Then we must help her heal herself."

"How does one help heal an old woman terrified of death?"

"I don't know. It won't be easy, but we've got to. I need this place and I don't want it to change."

"Your brownstone."

"Yes, my brownstone. It can't change. It mustn't!"

Thelma gave me a look, said nothing. Again, we slept separately; no thought of love.

# 24

IN THE PARLOR THE FOLLOWING MORNING, THE VASES that Julie had just scrubbed seemed smelly, and the fresh flowers almost drooped. The day was overcast, so the bits of glass hanging in the windows cast no patterns of light. The canaries were still silent, and the whole place gave off a sickeningly sweet whiff of decay. Or was I imagining it? I couldn't tell.

At nine a.m. I took a bowl of broth to Ida. I knocked and was told, "Come in." Entering, I placed the bowl on a table by the rocking chair. She was rocking slowly, hair down, her face as lined and naked as before.

"Thank you, Junius. You may go."

"Miz Ida, I hope you'll be coming downstairs soon. We need you."

She was sipping the broth, seemed to pay no attention.

"Miz Ida, my father was the best barber in this city, first for white folks, then for blacks. He used to tell me, 'Junius, whatever you do, be the best!' I've always tried to do that."

"You're the best butler I've ever had." She went on sipping the broth.

"Thank you. But what I want to say is this: in your occupation, you're far and away the best. The others can't even try to touch you. I'm proud to work for you; we all are. We don't want things to change."

"Change is inevitable. It creeps, it oozes. Like pus. I can smell it."

"Miz Ida, without you in the parlor it's just no go. Not one caller last night. We're losing business to the Seven Sisters."

At my mention of her rivals, Ida stopped sipping.

"They aren't sisters, Junius. They're scraped up from seven different gutters."

"Maybe so, ma'am, but they're stealing our customers. Which is a shame, because I've seen that block of theirs on Twenty-fifth Street at night: a jam of carriages, and long lines of men on the sidewalk waiting for a quick little romp inside. What the Sisters do clumsily and brazenly, you do discreetly, with style."

She pondered a moment, resumed sipping.

"And here's a bit of hot news: Restell is said to be parading around the Park in a shiny new equipage. Every eye is on her."

She looked straight at me, cannily. "Junius, are you deceiving me?"

"Only if you want me to, Miz Ida."

A faint smile. "The creature does crave attention, doesn't she?"

"But there's no way she could have matched our eighty-eight callers."

"Eighty-eight?"

"Eighty-eight. That's our final count."

"Hmm . . . Bring me the card receiver with the cards."

"I'll be glad to, Miz Ida."

Fetching it at once, I put it on the table. She was still sipping the broth when I left.

❧

Toward eleven she came downstairs in a house dress decked with braid, her face subtly powdered, her hair pyramided as usual.

"Eighty-seven," she announced as she passed me in the hall.

"Ma'am?"

"Eighty-seven cards, not eighty-eight."

I had forgotten to include Mr. Wash's, which was glittering on my dresser.

She went into the parlor, where I saw her smell the flowers in their vases, sound a single note on the pianoforte, tap a bronze Venus as if to make sure it was solid, touch marble, sniff brocade. After that she paced up and down for twenty minutes, then went to her desk in the library. Later, when she called me there to issue some routine instructions, I again noticed a stack of stock certificates of the Peoria & Pacific Railroad. She smiled.

"Junius, these certificates were a gift from Mr. Burns. I never spent a cent on his moonshine."

"That's no concern of mine, Miz Ida."

"The sanity of one's employer is always one's concern."

She lunched with the china dolls, whose conversation reverted to such matters as the chic of jet reticules and the growing importance of the bustle. Ida herself said nothing, then called for her carriage, went out.

At intervals during the morning Thelma and I had traded puzzled glances. Now, while Ida was out, I found myself alone in the parlor, sniffing the flowers again, feeling fabrics, touching bronze. Everything seemed clean, fresh, dry, and solid. Or did it?

Ida had gone out not done up to dazzle, as in outings to her bank or the Park, but dressed soberly for business. Why? Suddenly I grasped it: she was going to her lawyer to arrange the sale of the brownstone. Time indeed for the upstate mansion!

I almost panicked. I didn't want the upstate mansion; not now, when I was young and full of spunk. I'd feel smothered by all that tranquility.

I needed the city.

I needed the dark energy of its streets, with their hint of danger.

I needed the markets with their heaped melons and strung-up carcasses of beef, and the shrill cries of the vendors.

I needed the waterfront with its smells of brine and tar, and its hogsheads of tobacco being rolled up planks onto ships.

I needed the parade on the Drive in the Park of silver-harnessed turnouts thronged with fashionables eager to see and be seen.

I needed the Wash Burnses of the world, those frenzied, mindless doers racing toward elusive vistas of progress and power and wealth.

I needed the spectacle and comedy of Flash—that silly game they wouldn't let me play—and all the fakery sustaining it.

And as a refuge from the city's moil and toil, I needed my brownstone with its parlors of illusion contrived by an old woman, her stale flesh locked in whalebone, her cracked face caked with paint. I needed its damask and gilt, its hard bronze Venuses and brittle belles luring the lords of dominion, while the mirror-backed clock on the mantel ticked away the freshness of youth. I needed this place, with all its rich fictions and lies, as the setting, the fabulous setting, for my intimacies with Thelma, and to satisfy some deep need still not expressed, some wildness, some forbidden act, some final quirk of my obsession.

Ida returned at five, said nothing to anyone, went straight up to her room. At six, still in her house dress, she joined the china dolls for the usual light supper. "You will be in the parlor at eight," she informed them, then went back to her room; Thelma followed her upstairs. Since Dennis had accompanied Ida as groom on her outing, I hoped to get his report, but no opportunity arose. So, I too went up to my room and dressed for the evening, anticipating several more hours of listlessness, the girls glum, the callers few and mute.

On my way down the back stairs, I met Dennis, who anticipated my query.

"She went to all the better hotels and clubs, and had me leave a stack of these at each." He showed me a newly printed card:

**MADAM IDA'S**
**PRIVATE CLUB FOR GENTLEMEN**
**formal attire required**
**discretion assured**

And the address.

This did not suggest the selling of a brownstone. Hope surged, I squelched it; caution.

By eight o'clock the girls were all assembled in the parlor, splendidly got up, but numb. One canary was singing feebly; Ida had not appeared. Suddenly the knocker sounded. I hurried to the door, squinted through the peephole: a party of regulars, dressed to the nines, all sober, some with bouquets. I opened, waved them in.

Greeting them in the parlor was Ida, who had just come down, formidable in thick brocade, diamonds flashing, hair cascading in curls, skin marvelously smooth, wielding the inevitable eagle-feather fan. By what miracle had she transformed herself in so short a space of time?

Inspired by Ida, the conversation quickened, bouquets were presented to the girls, another bird or two started singing, the pianoforte sounded, more callers arrived, poignant poems were recited, and expensive drinks served. Then, as a chorus of canaries warbled, the company began discreetly breaking up into twosomes. Ida presided over all with a tight smile, assuring gray- and white-haired beaus, while beating the air with her fan, "This is the House of Youth." Buried for two days, on the third day she had risen.

# III

# 25

MY BROWNSTONE IS IN DANGER. FOUR YEARS HAVE passed since Mr. Wash's death and Ida's near retirement, ushering in the third and climactic phase of my obsession. In those four years everything has changed.

The city has changed. Boss Tweed has been arrested for corruption and his cronies routed by reformers. In 1873 a panic closed banks, demolished stocks, busted railroads, and plunged the city and the nation into the bleakest of depressions. Outside Ida's charmed interior, people are being evicted from brownstones, bankers are pawning diamonds, mills and furnaces lie idle, the unemployed are marching and rioting. "Velvets for a song!" scream the ads; no one buys. The lords of Tammany and Wall Street are laid low; Flash has flickered out.

In Ida's parlor the girls have been changed many times over, and the furnishings have been constantly renewed. Red carpets have been replaced by green ones, then blue, and stuffed birds have yielded to framed butterflies yielding to sea shells inscribed with scraps of poems ("Kisses make men loath to leave," etc.) in a frenzy that hints of desperation. Many of the old regulars have quit the scene, some as a result of the financial panic, and others by virtue of ailments or age. The survivors show up with graying or whitening locks, or dark hair lustrously dyed, some even shuffling on canes. They rub elbows now with dark-bearded governors of Western states and territories, ambassadors, congressmen, occasionally a French count or the son of an English baronet, since regardless of the times a visit to Madam Ida's has become a must for dignitaries passing through the city.

❧

Above all, Ida has changed. She is thinner now and walks with a cane. Her teeth are not her own; the fine fissures in her face are more pronounced. Thelma applies her makeup, combs and styles her hair, makes sure she inserts her dentures. "*I* am in charge of this brownstone!" she tells us repeatedly. "Yes, Miz Ida, of course," we always answer. Five minutes later she wonders where her purse is, or why the gas company is sending her a bill. Thelma or I accompany her to the bank, make sure she deposits the girls' earnings and her own. We keep her books, remind her to pay bills and give the staff their wages, coax from her a wavering signature when needed. We could take great advantage but we don't. The girls are becoming aware of her lapses; my vigilance keeps them in check. So far, because she's at her best in the parlor, the gentlemen callers seem not to have noticed. But for me the whole performance in the House of Youth, this creaking masquerade, comes off just short of grotesque. My second brownstone, like the first, is fast becoming a house of death.

Not all changes have been for the worse. With Ida's full blessing, Thelma and I were married three years ago in the Greater New Tabernacle Baptist Church, to Bessie and Dilly's delight. Since the bride had no living relatives, Dennis gave her away; Julie was her bridesmaid. Ida did not attend, but she supplied the wedding lavishly with flowers, and as a gift gave us all the furnishings that I had lifted from the storeroom to line my silken nest. Bessie gave us recipes; Dilly, a wedding quilt whose bright colors now alternate on our bed with the Bible quilt, making us feel doubly rich.

Thelma and I now share my room in the brownstone. She continues as Ida's maid but expects our first child in a matter of months. "You understand, Junius," Ida told me in a lucid moment, "that to have small children pattering about this establishment would be, to put it mildly, unthinkable. Of course we will work something out." She has talked of lodging us with John, who is now married to Marie, in the coach house—a makeshift arrangement that cannot serve for long.

Every August, taking Thelma with her, Ida still goes upstate for a breath of fresh mountain air. I take full advantage of her absence to revel in her silken bedstead, plunged in voluptuous fantasies. When they return, Thelma tells me how, en route, Ida has scouted out this or that town as a possibility for the upstate mansion, whose day must come, and soon.

"She takes me with her when she looks at houses. They're spacious and grand, with wide porches, and lots of grounds around them. We haven't found the right one yet, but next time we will. We can't put it off any longer."

"Can she make these decisions?"

"Sometimes, not always. I know what she wants; I'll help. When we're looking, does she ever get attention!"

"No questions asked?"

"None. They smell money."

Will Thelma and I go with her? Thelma is willing to, but I am not. It provoked our first real quarrel, and a fierce one.

"She needs me," said Thelma. "I can't desert her."

"And I need this city! I won't be buried among potted shrubs and mosquitoes in some hick town upstate!"

"It wouldn't be forever."

"I want my brownstone, and I want it *here* and *now!*"

"You're a slave to your brownstone! Well, you're not going to have it much longer. Get ready for a change!"

We didn't speak for two days. A slave to my brownstone? The very idea infuriated me. But maybe it was true.

Then Ida, in another of those hushed late-night confidences, looking anxious and vulnerable, informed me, "Junius, you and Thelma are my family—the only one I've got."

At last I grasped it. Surrounded by servants and china dolls, and sought out by legions of callers, Ida has no friends. I thought of Mrs. Hammond, so totally alone in her dying. Ida needs us—desperately. What a genius she has for binding us to her! I am wary of her, in awe of her, resent her, admire her. But I don't want to go upstate.

Ida tempts us cunningly. She has promised us half the top floor for ourselves, or perhaps a cottage on the grounds: more space for a family than we could ever have in the city. The furnishings of my nest would be transplanted there, along with most of the brownstone's contents, including those of the dusty storeroom, minus the bronze Venuses and fleshy nudes in oil. Up there the brownstone would be re-created as a residence of sumptuous propriety; I could still caress its surfaces, breathe its fragrances daily. A splendid setting for Ida's final game: living the rich lie of her respectability.

Will I help her live that lie? Maybe I won't have to, since Ida is courted by death. I see her death approaching, a gentleman sporting a bold red vest and a smile, with a hint of a taint of semen, his gentle jeweled hands reaching toward her throat. Behind him in the far, far distance, my own death lurks: a woman in a patchwork dress, wise in woman lore, her soft-touching hands smelling of ginger and garlic and camphor, content to carry me back at last to the clean, crisp air of mountains that in this life I have never seen. I will not resist.

If Ida has changed, so have I. Still the guardian of the gate and the best-known and best-paid butler in the city, I am four years older and detect the first faint lines of maturity, breeding bolder, more desperate fantasies, a heightened perception of decay. Waking dreams entice me. I see Ida laid out in state on her bed, with candles flickering and the entire household in mourning. I see her casket taken away by a black-plumed hearse, the mourners watching in silence, the women weeping into black silk handkerchiefs. I see a regally sumptuous bed, scented, smooth, and soft, awaiting an occupant. I see myself in that bed, reclining with the majesty of kings, Thelma lying beside me. And I rejoice: with Ida once and for all removed, ignoring legal niceties—my name in no deed or will—I achieve full possession at last. Be it only for weeks, days, hours, bed and brownstone are totally mine!

No obsession can ever go too far. In dreams I see Ida in her bed at night, old, tremulous, aware of soft footsteps approaching. She clutches for a silver bell just beyond her reach, then gapes in terror as two strong hands reach for her throat, tighten their fingers round it, squeeze; her eyes pop, she gasps. This little drama I ponder afterward in a cold sweat, heart thumping, having recognized those hands.

But wouldn't that be justice? By what right does Ida claim to own this brownstone? For her, it is only a money-making enterprise, a stage for her revenge and hate. She doesn't love its fabrics, breathe in its aromas, caress its marble, wood, and bronze. By what right does she leave its workings to others, whether the girls who service the clients, or the help who perform the gritty daily tasks of maintenance, while she plays queen of the realm? *By what right?*

Under all that whalebone and brocade, Ida is a shriveled old woman, the weakest of the weak; my hands are firm and strong. Mr. Wash said *dream, dare, do.* For years I have dreamed. Isn't it time to dare and do?

My dreams go further still. I see the magnificent bedstead on fire, flames lapping at the carved mahogany posts, devouring the rose-colored damask hangings, the counterpane of blue brocade. I see the parlor with its rich carpeting and velvets and silks, its crystal chandeliers, its busty Venuses and bibelots, all engulfed in an inferno that reduces them to charred timber, cinders, and ash. If I cannot totally possess them, neither shall anyone else. Sometimes Ida reclines in her bed, helpless, as the flames consume it. Sometimes I myself am a witness of this conflagration, glorying in it; sometimes, terrified, I am trapped in its midst. Afterward, jolted back into reality, I am shaken, bewildered, dazed.

"But these are only dreams," I assure Thelma and myself, "the robustious dreams of obsession."

"Damn your obsession!" she explodes. "I'm jealous of it as I'll never be jealous of a woman. It corrupts you, it leads you astray!"

"It tells me who I am."

"So much the worse for us both! It's got you wallowing in thoughts of murder and arson and suicide."

"You'll admit it has a cold, clean logic of its own."

"You're a fool at times, Junius, but you aren't a thief, an arsonist, or a murderer. So, shake free from these dreams."

"I need them! They round me out."

"You can't have them and me. I won't live with a man who's lost in fantasies—and dangerous fantasies at that. Them or me: which?"

"Both!"

"No! You've got to choose!"

The logic of dream against the logic of reality. Magnificence and risk and daring against Thelma and the scrape of dry, hard fact. Which?

❧

Lester Hicks has fallen again from on high. With Mr. Wash's death, the value of Lester's Peoria & Pacific shares plummeted; the panic wiped him out. Mr. Wash's widow kept him on as groom, but Lester, being flat broke, sold his gig, and had creditors snapping at his heels. While doing an errand for Ida, I ran into him and Rosalie on Broadway. They were looking at the lavish window displays at Tiffany's: bronze statuettes, jeweled clocks and paperweights, silver goblets, fancy fans—all the glitter and fripperies of Flash. My greeting surprised them, and I sensed a trace of chagrin. I had caught them looking at a shop they couldn't set foot in, and whose offerings they could never afford. I too had looked at it once, wanting to hurl a brick through the window, but they showed only yearning and chagrin.

Diverted from the window, Lester struck a new note. "I'm restless, Junius. I've heard there are black cowboys out West. I feel a great yearning for gulches and mesas and Big Sky. Unless I work as a waiter on a Hudson River steamboat; they're said to be palatial."

"I ain't aiming to be a cowgirl," said Rosalie. "And no wife to a cowboy either!" Her blue dress looked a bit worn, as did Lester's unpolished boots and jacket.

"Easy, little artichoke," said Lester. "We'll work something out."

"Like what?"

"I'll think of something."

"You'd better."

Weeks later he came to me at Ida's, disheveled, distraught. The girls weren't down yet; I talked to him briefly in a side room.

"She's gone! She's deserted me!"

"Your artichoke? Your sine qua non?"

"Vanished! Not even a good-bye note! Just when I needed her most!"

"I'm sorry, Lester."

"Maybe she was right, Junius. Rats desert a sinking ship. I'm foundering, I'm plunging to the depths."

"I doubt it. Drifting a bit, not sinking."

"Junius, there's nothing here by way of jobs. Can you see me as a janitor, a laborer?"

"Not your style at all."

"And even those jobs are hard to get, especially if you're black."

"What about being a cowboy under the Big Sky?"

"I couldn't get out there. I'm broke."

"Or a waiter on a palace steamboat?"

"No openings. And if I did get a job, my creditors would grab all my wages. They dog my every step."

"Your imagination will save you. It always has."

"Not this time, Junius. Humankind can only take so much. This is it. The end, the bitter, bitter end."

With that, he left, deep in a deep blue funk. He hadn't even asked me for money.

A month later a man answering to Lester's description burst into the pilot house of a Jersey-bound ferry, thrust a sealed note at the pilot, and slipped away into the throng of commuters. Minutes later, with the ferry safely berthed in Jersey City, the pilot opened the note and read it:

"Life is a botheration. I depart it gladly, wishing better times to my friends, and the pox to my creditors.—Lester Odysseus Hicks."

Just then a crewman noticed a felt bowler and a tasseled walking stick floating in the river; retrieved, they were identified as Lester's. The body was never found. Since then the river has frozen over, so Lester is either locked in its depths or floating under a thick sheet of ice, adrift in death as in life. When spring comes and the ice loosens and cracks up, and surges downstream into the harbor and out into the vast Atlantic, it will carry, along with crumpled small craft and broken bridges and pier ends, Lester's thawed remains. Unless spotted and recovered, they will be deposited among sharks and octopi in the ocean's deepest deeps. A fitting end to an adventurous life.

So the press has advised us, having chronicled his disappearance briefly, but I don't believe it for a minute. Lester wouldn't do away with himself; he loves life much too much. He faked suicide to escape his creditors. Sooner or later, under his own name or another, he'll be seen again on these streets, launching yet another career. He's a modern Odysseus (I've been reading up on mythology), but at the end of his wanderings no Penelope or Ithaca awaits him.

❧

Am I a thief, an arsonist, and a murderer, or just an intoxicated dreamer? Forced by Thelma to decide, I decided. A dreamer, of course: wild, inspired, desperate, but a dreamer, a mere dreamer, nonetheless. And that won't do. So, I have chosen the logic of reality, or maybe it has chosen me. Ida can rest easy, her fragile throat intact, her rich furnishings unsinged, uncharred, and safe. I've told Thelma that I'll go with her and Ida to the upstate mansion and re-create my brownstone there. A tamer, safer brownstone, where I will live quietly, free from desperate dreams. With the city in the grip of a depression, tranquility may, for a while, have its charm. But the real game will be something else.

"We must help her with her dying," I tell Thelma.

"Is she dying?"

"Slowly. That's what going up there is all about."

"What can we do?"

"Cure her of her illusion."

"The illusion of youth?"

"No. The illusion of control."

This is where my obsession has finally brought me: amid sumptuous furnishings, but feeling sober and diminished, to help a selfish, half-doting old woman let go of these spoils of whoredom, and the bitterness that led her to them, so she can walk free and naked into whatever mansion awaits her after death. It won't be easy; she clutches.

And what if Ida, having no heirs, willed her property to us? Unlikely, yet not inconceivable. A possibility—wild, provocative—that Thelma and I refuse to contemplate.

❧

My obsession has had its excesses—glorious excesses—but without it what would I have been? A puny little aimless man. From now on I shall try to live small, but not too small, not too puny or aimless, well aware that, on occasion, an obsession can go too far.

Mr. Wash was pushy and coarse. What redeemed him? His obsession, his need to go and go. *Destiny. Dream, dare, do: America!* Is this real? Is this illusion? I don't know. But it's Go Ahead, it keeps us pushing on.

This city is a cauldron of obsessions; that is its fascination.

Restell's obsession, still seen daily, is to flaunt herself in the teeth of public opinion. Dangerous; I admire her.

Ida's obsession is her hatred of men and her need for vengeance. It has taken her far, at a cost.

Lester has no obsession, only spurts and whims. In spite of all his talents—imagination, energy, gift of spiel—he drifts.

Thelma has no obsession, doesn't need one. She is my link to the real, my sanity, my repose.

Our children will not be bland. Wherever they grow up, I want them to know this city, its energy and danger. I want them to know Go Ahead and the cost of Go Ahead. I want them to dream, dare, do, have anger when anger is needed, and calm, cold calm, when calm is required. I want them to have rich obsessions, but to know the difference between fantasy and fact. I want them to be bold and wild, knowing and wise. I want them to be free.

**I hope you enjoyed this book as much as I enjoyed writing it. Would you do me a favor?**

We authors rely on online reviews to encourage future sales. Your opinion really matters. Please take a few minutes to give your opinion of my book at the review site of your choice. Amazon is especially useful, if you bought it there. Be honest, and remember that a review can be only a paragraph long, or a sentence or two, or even just one word.

Many thanks.

# Acknowledgment

I would like to thank the team at WiDo Publishing for helping to make this book happen. Throughout the whole process they were wonderfully diligent and patient.

# About the Author

Clifford Browder is a writer living in New York City's Greenwich Village high above the Magnolia Bakery of "Sex and the City" fame. He loves New York for its intensity and diversity, its craziness and creativity, and celebrates it, warts and all, in his blog, "No Place for Normal: New York."

Browder's published works include biographies of the Wall Street financier Daniel Drew and the notorious abortionist Madame Restell, three nonfiction titles about New York and New Yorkers, and a critical study of the French Surrealist poet André Breton.

*Forbidden Brownstones* is the fifth title in his Metropolis series of historical novels set in nineteenth-century New York. The other works in the series are *The Pleasuring of Men,* about a respectably raised young man who decides to become a male prostitute, servicing the city's elite; *Bill Hope: His Story,* in which a young street kid turned pickpocket tells of his misadventures, including escape from prison in a coffin; *Dark Knowledge,* about a young man who is appalled to learn that his family may have been involved in the illegal pre–Civil War slave trade, and sets out to learn the truth; and *The Eye That Never Sleeps,* in which the detective hired to apprehend the thief plundering the city's banks develops a strange friendship with his chief suspect. Browder researches his novels thoroughly, using primary sources whenever possible.

Browder has never owned a car, a television, or a cell phone, barely tolerates his computer, and eats garlic to fend off vampires. (So far, it seems to be working.)

CPSIA information can be obtained
at www.ICGtesting.com
Printed in the USA
LVHW112042281220
675236LV00007B/1683

9 781947 966420